OTHER NOVELS BY
DAVID L. SIMMONS

The Last Matriarch: Day of the Robin

The Last Matriarch: Bob White

The Fishbowl

GIP

A Fishbowl Novel Based on an FBI Program

To DR. Patel best wishes and many blessings David Simmons '022

DAVID L. SIMMONS

ARCHWAY
PUBLISHING

Archway Publishing books may be ordered through booksellers or by contacting:

Archway Publishing
1663 Liberty Drive
Bloomington, IN 47403
www.archwaypublishing.com
844-669-3957

Because of the dynamic nature of the Internet, any web addresses or
links contained in this book may have changed since publication and
may no longer be valid. The views expressed in this work are solely those
of the author and do not necessarily reflect the views of the publisher,
and the publisher hereby disclaims any responsibility for them.

Any people depicted in stock imagery provided by Getty Images are
models, and such images are being used for illustrative purposes only.
Certain stock imagery © Getty Images.

ISBN: 978-1-6657-2195-0 (sc)
ISBN: 978-1-6657-2194-3 (hc)
ISBN: 978-1-6657-2193-6 (e)

Library of Congress Control Number: 2022906980

Print information available on the last page.

Archway Publishing rev. date: 04/08/2022

ACKNOWLEDGMENTS

Dr. Ben Wright at the University of Maryland in Europe

Dr. Elvin Hope at Texas State University at San Marcos

Rev. Dr. A. Knighton Stanley and his daughter Katheryn Stanley, for his inspiring book *A View from My Window*

To Joseph Taylor Stanley, A. Knighton Stanley, Henry
T. Simmons, and all Southern Christian Leadership
Conference activists.

PROLOGUE

In 1967, George Dorsette was kicked out of the Ku Klux Klan. The reason for his dismissal? He was considered an informant for the Federal Bureau of Investigations. The KKK figured that their movements had been monitored and that their days were numbered.

A conniving soul escaped from Missouri State Penitentiary. He fled to Canada but was unable to make his way to Africa. As a backup plan, he drove to Alabama, and then to Mexico. He stayed there before he made his way to Los Angeles in November 1967. After lying low, he left California in March 1968.

> Jesus asked him, are you betraying the Son of Man with a kiss?
>
> —Luke 22:48 (KJV)

CHAPTER 1

NW District of Columbia, Fourteenth Street.

A fire truck whined as it maneuvered through traffic in the Shaw neighborhood. China Lee King—known as "Stick" for his lanky frame—waited outside of Crown Pawnbrokers. When Sam Yoke stepped out, the necklace he had bought glistened.

"Can't believe you bought a crucifix from a pawn shop," Stick said. "Who buys dead folks' stuff?" He paused and looked away. "You, that's who."

Yoke looked smugly at him. It would be a waste of time to explain his actions. Yoke worked on Capitol Hill. He wasn't a Howard University student, and he had no desire to be one. Coming from the ghetto to become a Capitol Hill janitor was a big deal for him. He reveled in having access to information that affected Black folks. All the inappropriate ethics he had witnessed on Capitol Hill made the crucifix small potatoes. But Stick was different. He was gullible.

Stick was a guard on the Howard University basketball team. A professional scout regarded him as a promising prospect, so he bombarded him with perks. As a result, Stick never worried about picking up the check for a meal, paying for clothes, or even going to class.

It was Friday evening on the Ides of March 1968. Yoke and Stick headed for a men's clothing store on Fourteenth called Cavaliers.

As they walked, Yoke browsed storefront windows and said, "Man, do you need it."

Stick towered above most pedestrians. "Should've seen all those fly cats at the CIAA Tournament," he said. "They were clean. All those fur coats, slick suits, and fancy cars forced me to do something with my loose change."

"Man, Howard hasn't won since 1912. Watch yourself. All of them aren't there to help. Eventually, someone will want something in return. See it all the time on Capitol Hill."

"That could be a good thing," Stick replied. "One hand washes the other."

They strolled into Cavaliers, where Otis Redding's "(Sittin' On) The Dock of the Bay" played over an intercom. A young man said, "Can I help you?"

Stick said to him, "Want to buy that leather trench coat."

A young woman walked over and said to Stick, "May I help you?" Stick looked at the young man as the woman again asked, "May I help you?"

The young man looked toward the entrance, looked around, and said, "Sure, let me get it."

Yoke whispered to Stick, "That guy doesn't work here."

Stick walked with the woman to the leather coats' rack and got the trench coat. He put it on in front of a mirror and said, "Told you it's fly."

Yoke said, "Looks like you're spending the money before you make it."

"It's only a bill and a quarter," Stick said as he posed in the mirror. He took it off and went to the register. He paid the clerk, and they left for the shoe store.

Stick said as they walked into Hahn Shoes, "Flat-sole shoes are out of style." He looked at the line of platform boots from New York.

"My Chuck Taylors are cool. Why do you feel you have to shell out money to look good?"

"College gives no guarantee you'll get a job, but pro scouts can. Especially the Seventy-Sixers."

"I pray you make the roster," said Yoke.

Stick tried on a suede platform boot. "Has nothing to do with prayer. It's all about skill. I average twenty-one points. If Monroe can make it, I can too."

"What about Bobby Dandridge or Soapy Adams? They're in the running."

"Thanks for worrying about them," Stick said as he made an imaginary free throw. "It takes the pressure off."

They walked to the counter. Stick paid for the suede boots, and they left.

As they walked on Fourteenth, Yoke said, "A strange thing happened at work today."

"What? You found a clean mop?" said Stick.

Yoke said curtly, "Think you're smart, huh? No. Two men in dark suits got our roster and took it to my supervisor."

"What's strange about that?"

"The roster is confidential. Those guys must have a clearance to even look at it. Not only did they look at it—they scanned the roster and pointed at a name."

"So?"

"They pointed close to my name."

Yoke and Stick stood on the corner of Fourteenth and U as traffic on U rolled through the intersection. Stick said, "There you go. Every time something is missing, blame the Black man."

"Haven't stole anything," said Yoke. "At least not as much as those politicians. I may grab a pen or a donut, but nothing of value. We all do that. And they know it."

"What do you think they wanted?"

"Don't know."

U Street traffic rolled to a stop, and then Fourteenth traffic started to proceed.

"But earlier today," Yoke said, "while I was putting toilet paper in the men's restroom, two congressional aides came in talking 'bout it's Tennessee turn."

"What did they say?" Stick asked as they crossed U Street.

"When they saw me, they clammed up and waited until I left."

"You're probably overreacting."

"Maybe you're right," said Yoke. "Being around those politicians can make you paranoid. It's like they pass laws to keep us down. The Voting Rights Act was an exception. And the only reason it passed was the Democrats needed to beef up their numbers of registered voters."

"Relax and enjoy your weekend. Hang out with me tonight. There's a party not far from Howard."

"Okay, but the moment someone start using ten-dollar words, I'm going to jive them down."

Stick laughed as they stood at the bus stop. "Most of the guys play ball. But the honeys that will be there, who knows?"

*   *   *

Meanwhile, in the 2200 block of Fourteenth, Melba and her roommate were walking. Outside 2204 Fourteenth Street, young ladies waited.

As they got closer, Melba said to her roommate, "Just listen. Don't cause no friction. Everything will be fine. It's better than waiting on tables."

A gleaming Cadillac pulled in front of the row house. The way the driver climbed out suggested she had to be close to fifty. Odessa Madre parted the ladies as she walked to the door. Melba and her roommate strolled behind the ladies as they followed Odessa inside the house known as Club Madre.

They went into a room where there was a table with twelve long-stemmed roses in the center. After they entered, the Queen, as she was known by those in her circle, sat, and the ladies followed. She said, "Came here on a mule wagon; the last time I went to Georgia, I was in a Cadillac." She looked around and was mindful to look each lady in the eye. "In this town, if I can do it, you can too." She looked at the new lady. "Who you?"

"Kaseya Ford, ma'am."

Odessa returned her attention to the rest of the ladies. "Now, let's get ready for tonight."

It was at that moment that Kaseya realized this job was more than pouring liquor. It was about the unpredictable street life. Yet it was better than Logan Circle.

Odessa got up. "Melba, you and Kaseya stay." She walked over to Kaseya and sat on the table. "You have 'virgin' written all over you. What's your story?"

"My full name is Kaseya Connie Ford. When my mother was angry with me, instead of calling me Kaseya Connie, she settled for Kaseya, which means KC. I was born and raised in northwest DC."

Odessa said, "Me too. This neighborhood was called Cowtown. Negroes and Irishmen got along real well. If the Italian or German kids came to fight the Irish, Negroes would chuck bricks at them. It was called the Great Rock Chucking Wars." She stood. "I grew up with men who have become captains, lieutenants, and even superintendents in the police department. That's who protects us."

Kaseya looked up at Odessa. "Right now, I live on Missouri Avenue," she said. "I graduated from a private school and worked in the Department of Commerce."

"Why are you here? That's a good job."

"Well, a man got mad at me when I refused to sneak around. He lied on me, and that got me fired."

Odessa had heard that story before. That's why she had a soft heart for young ladies who had been lied to by sleazy men. "Well, Kaseya, life is too short to live broke. Crime does pay. Is it worth it? You can make a hell of a lot of money. There're always larcenous hearts who're gonna listen to you. And when you show 'em that money, that wad, they'll suck up to you like you was a Tootsie Roll. Don't let anyone tell you different. You don't pull on Superman's cape, you don't spit in the wind, you don't tug the mask off the Lone Ranger, and honey, you don't mess with Odessa. Okay? I may be old, and I may be ugly, but I ain't dumb. That's why I'm the Queen." She turned to Melba. "She's not ready to be a pro. She'll start out working the floor. Show her the ropes." She then said to Kaseya, "No drugs. Everybody knows I can't stand them reefers. You'll have Sundays off. And, if you're loyal, you can relax on my porch."

"Yes ma'am. Thanks, Miss Odessa," said Kaseya. They got up and walked into the club room.

* * *

Row houses 2000 thru 2004 on U Street were built by Frederick Douglass. Yoke chose to live in 2002 for that reason. Yoke arrived at his apartment and noticed a bland government car.

He checked his apartment mailbox and climbed the stairs to his apartment. When he went inside his apartment and looked through his front window, he saw two dark-suited men get out and walk to the main entrance. It wasn't long before he heard them ascend the stairs. There was a knock at his neighbor's apartment. Yoke was ready to surrender. He wanted to extinguish the anguish that had haunted him all day. He figured they were at the wrong apartment, so he opened his front door and saw the men with drawn pistols next door.

One man yelled, "Don Settles, this is the FBI. Open up!"

Settles opened his door, and the men went inside. After a few minutes, the FBI agents emerged with two grenades and placed them in an evidence bag. One FBI agent said, "Thanks for your cooperation, Mr. Settles. It will be noted." The men walked past Yoke and descended the stairs. He closed his door.

Now, Yoke thought about Don Settles being a Vietnam veteran and had shown him two grenades he had brought back from the war. Since Don was a student at Howard under the GI Bill. Yoke guessed that the FBI considered Don non-hostile and decided not to take him downtown.

Yoke went straight to his bedroom and laid his packages on the bed. Pressed for time, he went straight to the bathroom to run his bath water, but a knock at the door forced him back to the living room. Before he opened it, he figured the FBI agents were back to deal with him. He turned the doorknob, and his dark-skinned supervisor, Mr. Peak Smith, said, "Had to stop. We need to talk."

"Talk about what?" Yoke asked in a puzzled manner. "Come in."

He moved with the blistering speed of a turtle and sat at a drop-leaf tea table next to the bay window.

The middle-aged Mr. Smith said, "You did something today, and I need to know."

"Well, sir, I don't know what I did."

Mr. Smith said, "This afternoon I was told to come and tell you to report to FBI Headquarters Monday morning at 8:00 a.m. You'll see Agent Victor Kent."

"Wait, I haven't done anything wrong. Someone has to be lying."

Mr. Smith went on. "He's from an upper-crust family in Richmond, Virginia. He graduated from Penn State, and after he finished his internship at the FBI, he graduated from Gee Dub School of Law."

"Who told you?"

Mr. Smith said, "Son, on Capitol Hill it's crucial you make alliances. My job is not only to supervise; I'm tasked to assess personnel and provide recommendations to other agencies. But in your case, I was forced to compromise." Mr. Smith paused. "Sometimes we hear things but don't know what we heard. Sometimes we see things but don't recognize what we saw. Sometimes we say things and don't realize who we are talking to. Now I need to know what you heard today. And please don't lie."

Yoke knew Mr. Smith's mind was malignant from how things worked on Capitol Hill. Mr. Smith never asked a question if he didn't know the answer. Yoke said, "Well, sir, in the men's restroom, I heard an aide say, 'It's Tennessee turn …' He clammed up when he saw me."

Mr. Smith said, "What did you see today?"

"Saw two men look at our roster and then talk to you."

"When one man was talking to me," said Mr. Smith, "did you notice the other man looking at you?"

"No."

"Well, son, he was," said Mr. Smith. "They had a description of you that included that dust mop you carry in your back pocket."

Yoke said as he looked at the floor, "Haven't done anything wrong. We hear things all the time, and they come to you all the time."

"This time it's different," said Mr. Smith. "Now, who did you tell?"

"Told Stick I thought it was strange. And you coming here proves me right."

Mr. Smith said, "You know you're not to discuss anything that's done on Capitol Hill. Consider yourself admonished."

Yoke supplied no rebuttal.

Mr. Smith said, "I had to know before I tell you this." He paused. "Working on Capitol Hill is like working in a fishbowl. You're watched more than you know, even if you're just another fish."

"Why do I have to see them?"

Mr. Smith sighed as he stood and walked toward the door. He said with remorse, "Think of it this way: You're Samson and he's the Philistine army. Use your jawbone and talk your way out." He paused. "Just do as you're told. And remember: Never ask the one-word question 'Who?' And never ask 'What's going on?' Have a good weekend."

Yoke stood. "Yes sir." He watched Mr. Smith leave and thought, *What the hell?*

There's a saying in the espionage world: "The third man is always listening." That's what Yoke had just encountered, but he, like others, would soon learn the inevitable. Nothing can escape the fishbowl.

CHAPTER 2

That night The Temptations' *Wish It Would Rain* played as it rained ladies galore at a party over on Thirteenth. Most of the athletes ushered them to a makeshift bar. Others escorted them to a table holding a selection of finger foods used to soak up the alcohol. Stick and Yoke stood near an ice chest packed with beer.

Stick said, "This why I dress like I do." An attractive lady made her way to Stick, snuggled up, and kissed him. When their lips parted, he said, "Claire, this is Yoke."

She smiled.

Yoke nodded.

Stick said, "She won't give nobody that stuff but me. Ain't that right?"

She blushed, smiled embarrassedly, and purred, "That's right, baby."

He looked Yoke over and said, "You dress like an average Joe." Then he added, "What's wrong?"

"Nothing's wrong." Yoke declined to elaborate in fear of another admonishment. "Just don't feel right."

Stick said, "I know what you need. Let's go to Club Madre. She got ladies who can stimulate the dead."

* * *

At Club Madre, Kaseya sat alone at a table. Men came in and went straight to the ladies they wanted. It was as though attention was given to women who moved with an easy, loose strut. Some men felt those women's demeanors would better their chances to score.

Melba walked over to Kaseya and said, "You've got to move around. You know, break the ice and make friends."

Kaseya said, "I'll go to the bar and hang out there."

"Good," said Melba. "Now you're learning."

Stick and Yoke entered. "See what I mean?" Stick said. "Look at that hammer over there." He pointed at Melba.

Yoke was out just to ease his conscience. The ladies didn't move him. "Going to the bar," he said.

"I'm going over there."

Yoke walked over and stood at the bar. "Rum and Coke."

Kaseya said to him, "Kaseya Ford," and she laid a hand on his shoulder.

Taken by her innocence, he said, "Sam Yoke. Want a drink?"

"Sure," she said. "A tequila sunrise."

"There's something about you that makes you stand out." Her behaviors gave him the impression she must be expensive.

"Thanks, this is my first night here. Got fired from my last gig."

He said, "That bad, huh?"

"That bad," she said.

The bartender placed their drinks before them.

"Thanks," he said to the bartender, and he paid him.

She said after she took a sip, "Where do you work?"

"I'm a janitor on Capitol Hill."

She said, "That bad, huh?"

"Not really," he said. "I like it." *In spite of the fact I could lose my job Monday morning.* That thought hit him right in the gut.

She said, "Why do you look downhearted?"

"Oh, it's nothing. Just not up to it tonight."

"Neither am I," she said. "Can you escort me home?"

Yoke looked around. "Can't wait to blow this joint."

As they made their way out, Yoke said to Stick, "See you tomorrow at the gym."

Stick gave him a thumbs-up.

Melba followed them to the door and watched.

The moment Yoke and Kaseya stepped onto the sidewalk, a plainclothes officer stepped into their path.

He flashed a badge and said, "Metro Vice. Where are you headed?"

Kaseya said, "He's seeing me home."

"Yeah, right," said the officer.

Melba's smile dissolved. She went to Odessa and whispered into her ear. Odessa picked up the phone.

The officer's radio squelched erratically. "Don't move," he said. "I'm not finished." He went to his unmarked car.

After a moment, he returned and said, "Go home."

As they walked up Fourteenth, Kaseya said, "What are you doing Sunday?"

"Nothing, why?"

She said, "Come with me to church."

"Look, I don't have a phone. Why don't I meet you there?"

"Sure, meet me at People Church on Thirteenth Street at eleven."

"Got to be there. Thanks for making my night."

"Thanks for coming to my rescue," she said, and she kissed him on his cheek.

*   *   *

On Saturday during the wee hours in one of Club Madre's bedrooms, Stick lay on the bed while Melba cleaned him with a washrag. When she was finished, she went and cleaned herself. She returned and sat on the bed while he got dressed.

She said as she covered her breast with the sheet, "I see you all the time and was wondering when we would get together."

"Now you know," he said as he put on his shirt. "Who was that girl with Yoke?"

"Yoke? And which girl?"

"The guy that spoke to me and I gave a thumbs-up to." He stepped into his slacks.

She said, "Oh, that guy. He was with Kaseya. This was her first night."

"Thought she looked green," he said as he tucked in his shirt. "Where does she live?"

"With me. We're roommates. Don't ask where, because I'm not going to tell you. Let's keep it professional."

He said, slipping into his shoes, "this town is full of secrets."

"Where're you from?"

"Memphis, Tennessee. And you?" He tied his necktie.

"Silver Springs, Maryland."

"Well," Stick said, "guess I'll see you soon."

She called out seven numbers.

"What the hell that supposed to mean?" he said as he flung on his suit coat.

She said, "That's my phone number. Call me the next time you're coming. I'll wait."

"Sure," he said, and he left.

*　*　*

The basketball pinged as it bounced on the hardwood floor. Shoes squeaked as they hustled up and down the court. Howard's gym was full of activity that Saturday morning. It was routine for basketball players to work out during the off season. Stick vouched for Yoke even though he wasn't supposed to be on campus without proper permission. So far, the guys liked playing with and against him. At times, they wondered why he wasn't playing for some college.

When Yoke made a jump shot from the deep corner, Stick shouted, "Next!"

They sat in the bleachers while the next team warmed up.

Stick said over dribbling balls, "How did it go with Kaseya?"

"You know her?" said Yoke. Three balls hit the rim at the same time.

"Her roommate told me," Stick replied. "It may have been her first night, but that don't mean she doesn't want to be loved. Did you hit it?"

A tongue-flashing player looked at Stick as he dribbled between his legs.

"Grow up," said Yoke. "Even if I did, why you need to know? And you call me nosey."

"Just jiving. Lighten up, brother man. Know you're edgy. I'm trying to help."

Another player said to Stick, "Y'all ready?"

Yoke said to Stick, "Sorry, man. She's a nice girl. Supposed to meet her at church tomorrow."

"Wait!" Stick shouted to the other player. He laughed and said to Yoke, "Hope she don't sit too close to you. You'll kill her good reputation."

Balls resumed bouncing. Yoke said to Stick, "How can you talk? I don't have to guess how your night ended."

"Where does she live?" Stick asked.

"On Missouri."

Another player said to Stick, "Will y'all come on."

"Y'all need the practice," Stick said to him. "Now shut the hell up. Can't you see I'm busy?" He said to Yoke, "I was with her roommate. That's how I know Kaseya. But Melba wouldn't tell me where they live."

"Hell, I wouldn't either after I saw your snakehead."

Stick said, "Forget you, man. Feel better don't cha?"

"Feel all right," said Yoke. "I ran off a lot of tension in that game."

"Naw you didn't," said Stick, "You lost a lot of tension last night. Call me Doctor Stick. I know what to prescribe and how to heal." He closed his eyes, held his hands to the ceiling and said, "Thank ya Jesus!"

One of the players on the court said to Stick, "This isn't registration. Any day now."

Stick and Yoke stepped onto the court. Stick said, "Yoke, take the ball out."

*   *   *

Kaseya and Melba ate breakfast on a maple dinette table that sat at a front window.

"Tell the Queen I won't be back," said Kaseya. "I'm desperate for a job, but not that desperate."

"Think she'll understand," Melba replied. "I saw what she saw. That kind of work isn't for you. Who knows, you may get a job at another government department."

"Don't think I want to work up there. The guys are sleazy, the women are loose, and the bosses lie to your face. Want to work at a place where you get credit for what you do, not how you do 'em."

"Wake up! That's the real world. There's a price on everything no matter what. Either you pay or someone pays you."

"Learned a lot about myself last night," said Kaseya. "Yoke told me memories are just memories if you don't learn from them."

"What do you want to do? But don't take too long. You're my girl, but I need help on the rent."

"Don't worry; I qualify for unemployment. I want to sort out my life. Meeting Yoke changed things."

"What happened in your bedroom?"

"Nothing happened. And that's it," she said, "nothing. He's supposed to meet me at church tomorrow."

"Hope he brings a handkerchief," said Melba. "You always bawl your eyes out at service."

Kaseya got up from the table and sang as she danced the mashed potato: "I feel good ... I breakout ... in a cold sweat ... I got Yoke!"

Melba laughed. "Watch out, James Brown."

"Going to get myself together," said Kaseya. "Let's get dressed and go to the beauty parlor. Your hair looks a mess. That man messed your hair *up!* Who was he?"

"Stick King. Howard basketball star and Yoke's friend. Think he might be going pro next year."

"Playing for who?"

"Philadelphia Seventy-Sixers."

"Great, we can double date."

"As long it begins and end at Club Madre," said Melba.

* * *

Yoke made it a point to see his mother every Saturday morning. He sat at the kitchen table and tackled the grub she had prepared for him.

"Thanks for breakfast," he said. "How you're doing?"

His mother, Mrs. Cynthia Yoke, was a retired teacher. His father worked in construction. He died in the summer of '64. They had five children; Yoke was their third.

"You're welcome," she replied. "I'm doing fine. How was your week?"

It was the one question he didn't want to answer. "Most of the week was business as usual."

"And the rest?" she asked.

"Don't know what to say about it. Let's say strange."

She put her hands on her hips and ordered, "What did you do?"

"Really don't know," he said. "But I got admonished for talking to Stick."

"That's it? I've been admonishing you since your father died."

Here it comes, he thought, *that 'should've listened to me' speech.*

She went on. "Why didn't you go to college like your sister and brothers? If you would've listened to me, you'd be graduating in May."

"College isn't for everyone," he said, "It's for those with ambitions to lead. It's for those teacher's pets who are hand-picked. Let's face it, I'm too short for basketball, And I'm not that great of a student. I'm satisfied pushing a broom."

"You're afraid of responsibility. You have a purpose in life. God blesses you, and you turn around and give your blessings to the devil."

"Mom, what if I fail? Will you still think God blessed me?" He needed to know how she would feel if he got fired on Monday.

She said, "I don't think; I know he's blessing you. It's up to you to let him lead the way."

Yoke's faith withered every time he had to deal with Capitol Hill. He said, "I'm about to lose my job. Are you satisfied?"

"An admonishment doesn't mean you will lose your job," she said. "It means you've been warned. Just don't do it again anytime soon."

"You don't know those people. They'll smile in your face and stab you in the back. They intentionally keep you off balance. That way they can manage your thoughts, beliefs, and off-duty activities."

"What are you doing tomorrow?"

"Going to church," he said.

She veered from him, smiled, and said, "That's a good decision."

He neglected to tell her about Kaseya. The way he saw it, even she was not a sure thing.

*   *   *

Stick, Melba and Kaseya were waiting at Ben's Chili Bowl on U Street.

Melba said, "Are you sure he's coming? I got to be at Club Madre at six."

"Stop worrying," Stick said. "He'll be here."

Kaseya's eyes searched in both directions. She believed it would be pure luck for her to see him before Sunday.

"You should've told him we're waiting," said Melba.

"Look," said Stick, "he's down on his luck. Kaseya may be the one who can help him snap out of it."

Yoke walked from around the corner off Fourteenth onto U. He had a feeling Stick was going to pump him for information. As much as he wanted to, he couldn't share it, even if talking about it would make him feel better. He spotted Stick standing tall above people in front of Ben's. As he got closer, he recognized Kaseya as she stood next to the alley.

"We been waiting," Stick said. "Why you got to be on colored people time?"

Yoke said to Kaseya, "Didn't expect to see you today."

She pointed at Melba. "This my roommate, Melba."

Yoke bowed enough for Melba to accept his acquaintance.

"Let's go grab a table," said Stick.

They went in and sat at a table for four. Yoke and Stick went to the counter.

Kaseya said to Melba, "He looks even better in sunlight."

"Looks can be deceiving," Melba replied. "I should know."

"To see my man when I wanted to makes this special."

Stick paid for the orders with bills pulled from a wad. Yoke took the orders to the table. It wasn't long before Stick joined them.

Yoke said to Kaseya, "This is a surprise. You made my day."

"Trying to ease your mind," she said. "You don't have to worry about me. Looking forward to church tomorrow."

They finished the grilled split chili dogs, fries, and sodas. Stick and Melba stood, and Stick said, "Going to go with Melba to Club Madre."

Yoke looked at Kaseya and said, "Aren't you going with them?"

"No," she replied, "Don't want to go there anymore."

Yoke said to Stick, "See you later."

Melba and Stick walked out. Kaseya glanced at Yoke. "Know it's none of my business, but what's bothering you?"

"Can't talk about it," said Yoke. "All I can tell you is you're beautiful without lipstick."

"Thank you. You're handsome for a janitor."

He needed her in his life—now. Butterflies fluttered in his gut. A couple of days ago, he had no worries. Now he existed with a troubled mind. He could fake it with her, but the truth of the matter is that he was scared as hell.

As for Kaseya, things weren't much better. She was unemployed. In a way, they were in the middle of the same storm. At that moment, church was only a prayer.

"Can I see you home?" Yoke asked.

"No," she said, "I've got a better idea. Let's go to the mall."

"Let's go." They got up and left.

*   *   *

Kaseya and Yoke walked beside the reflecting pond with the Lincoln Memorial in view.

"Why did you refuse to go to Club Madre?" Yoke asked

"Don't want to make money that way. I'll find another job."

"Where were you working before?"

"At the Department of Commerce," she said.

"Why did you quit?"

"I didn't," she said. "I was fired."

Fear once again entered his stomach. "Why?"

"Early last week, I could do no wrong at work. My supervisor claimed I was 'cooking with gas.' A White supervisor, from another section, started making passes. At times, when no one was watching, he would pat my rump."

Yoke said, "You should've yelled, 'Stop!' He would've been embarrassed."

"I didn't because he's married. Don't want to be the reason someone broke up. Anyway, he started letting me know where he was going and asked me to be there. I refused. One day his wife came to the office. While she was waiting, a coworker told me he had said he had an hour to burn and had asked me to meet him at a hotel. His wife heard it. So when she saw him, all hell broke loose."

"That's no reason to fire you," Yoke said.

"No, but it's what his wife heard and her husband's advances that got me in trouble. His wife cursed me up and down. To save face, he assured her I was coming onto him and I paid for the room. That's why I got fired."

By now, the Lincoln Memorial was twice as big.

"Because she's White," Yoke said. "They'll do anything, including lie, to keep them happy."

"But I heard they're swingers. So now I'm waiting to collect unemployment. But until I start getting it, I got to do something for money. But not Club Madre."

Yoke was enlightened. He believed she was someone he could count on if he got fired. He said, "It's amazing how they say something and everybody assume it's true."

They stood by the pond, with the memorial high and wide in front of them.

"Why are you down?" She asked.

"I can't tell you," said Yoke. "I was admonished for telling Stick. But I can tell you this: they transferred me to another building because I think someone lied on me. I could lose my job."

"That bad huh?"

"That bad."

"They're something else," she looked at her watch and said. "I got to go home."

"Okay. I'll see you home to make sure you're safe."

They had planned their date without knowing they were a day away from a refreshing oasis—People Congregational United Church of Christ.

*   *   *

Howard University's academic cultural stimulus in Crown Heights drifted into nearby neighborhoods. The Petworth neighborhood avowed it was a community called by faith, led by hope, and unified by love. At the intersection of Crittenden Street and Thirteenth Street NW was People Congregational United Church of Christ.

Sunday morning at ten forty-five, after a twenty-minute stroll, Kaseya waited at the church doors. Yoke walked strongmindedly for nearly an hour from U Street to Thirteenth. He went unwaveringly to her at the doors and said, "How long have you been waiting? We agreed on eleven, but I couldn't wait."

She looked at him and said with candor, "Couldn't wait either." She smiled.

"Who's the preacher?" asked Yoke.

"Pastor A. Knighton Stanley," she said, "He's been here a little over a month. Heard he's a civil rights activist, but to me, he pushes education. He's a good pastor."

They walked into the sanctuary where multicultural members were scattered throughout the pews. She leaned to Yoke's ear and whispered, "The stained-glass windows are by Dr. David Driskell."

Yoke noticed that the center pews were flanked by pews slanted toward the altar. They sat in one of the side pews, where Yoke got a good view of Pastor Stanley. He was a light-skinned man of average height. If he had played football, he would have been a running back. Then Yoke saw a stout, bow-legged man with a woman walk down the aisle and sit on the second pew.

It wasn't too long before the call to worship began … Pastor Stanley moved to the pulpit, and greeted the congregation, "So, we are many, one body in Christ… Roman twelve five King James Version. The title of today's word is The Faces of God …"

After the service, Kaseya led Yoke out and was stopped by the bowlegged man. He said to her, "Your eyesight must be going bad." He looked at Yoke and then said to her, "This one is good looking."

She laughed. "Aw, Brother Ward, he's my new friend."

"Y'all stay blessed," said Brother Ward.

Both faced a week of possible mayhem. To Kaseya, the sermon restored hope. As for Yoke, he had acquired strength through faith and was ready to tangle with his Philistines.

CHAPTER 3

Monday at 7:30 a.m., it was rain-cloud-dark-thirty when Yoke stepped off the bus. As soon as he reached the glass doors of FBI Headquarters, it poured. He walked with weak knees through a spacious foyer. By the time he reached the reception desk, his legs trembled.

A middle-aged receptionist sat at the reception desk. Her brunette hair was well groomed, and her fingernails were polished. She wore a conservative dress and spoke properly when she asked, "How can we help you?"

Yoke was smitten with the courtesy, but it didn't help him recapture the faith he had forsaken. He said, "I have an eight o'clock appointment to see Agent Victor Kent."

"One moment please." The receptionist picked up the phone. "Thank you, sir." She hung up. "He'll be down momentarily."

Yoke waited until he was tapped on the shoulder from behind. He faced a frosty-haired, dark-suited man who appeared to have well-earned authority. His mild tan left no question regarding his high life.

The man said with a harsh voice, "I'm Mr. Kent. You must be Sam Yoke."

"Yes sir, I am."

The receptionist held out a visitor badge and said to Yoke, "You must be escorted at all times. Should you get separated, stay where you are. We'll have someone escort you back to this desk. Do you understand?"

"Yes, I do."

"Good," said Mr. Kent. "Follow me." He turned and walked with unfaltering equilibrium.

They walked down a corridor at a steady pace that made it difficult to read or see what was hung on the walls. Halfway down the corridor, they turned right. A janitor pushing a dry mop broom looked at Yoke and then continued. They reached the office of the director of services. Written underneath the office title was "Mr. Victor Kent."

Mr. Kent opened the door and said to Yoke, "Have a seat." When he rounded his desk, he looked out the window and sang, "Rain, rain, go away. Come again another day."

His office was bland: no family pictures, no papers scattered over the desk, not even a jar of mints. Behind his desk were a library of operation manuals. There were yellow in-house messenger envelopes in a basket labeled "Outgoing." On the wall were sayings from famous people.

Mr. Kent turned from the window and sat. He opened a drawer and retrieved a folder. The moment he laid it on his desk, he examined the contents and mumbled, "Okay. Uh huh."

Yoke sat straight, but his spirit of security had dissolved.

Mr. Kent read aloud: "Samuel Douglas Yoke, a.k.a. Yoke. Born in 1946 to widow, my condolences, Mrs. Cynthia Yoke. No felonies, misdemeanors, and not even a parking or speeding ticket. Do you drive?"

"No."

"Didn't think so. If you had a college degree, joining the FBI would be a piece of cake."

Mr. Kent embellished. Having no degree was a good reason not to hire him. He continued, "Known Recent Associates: China Lee King, a.k.a. Stick. Born in Memphis, Tennessee, in 1946. Student basketball player at Howard University."

Yoke got nervous at the thought that Stick was under investigation for accepting money from boosters and not reporting it.

Mr. Kent went on, "Kaseya Connie Ford. You just met her. So, it's up to you to find out more about her. I'm not going to tell you." He closed the folder, looked at Yoke, and said, "Do you know why you're here?"

"No."

Mr. Kent stared at Yoke. "We know all about you and anyone else. For example, Stick keeps a pocket full of money. And you know it. Who gives him money? And don't lie." He tapped on the folder.

"Don't know. Never seen anyone give him money."

"Is that's why Mr. Smith admonished you?"

"No sir, he admonished me for talking to Stick about what happens on Capitol Hill."

"I know," Mr. Kent replied. "You were at Club Madre Friday night. Were there plenty of young ladies there?"

"Yes, sir."

Mr. Kent said, "Did Kaseya introduce you to the Queen?"

"No, sir," he said. *Is this about the Queen?*

"I know," said Mr. Kent. "She didn't show up for work Saturday night. Where were you going when you left with Kaseya?"

"I was seeing her home, sir."

Mr. Kent said, "Did she offer her services for money?"

"No. We didn't discuss sex."

A break in the clouds caused sunlight to shine through the window.

"Think you and her will make a nice couple," said Mr. Kent. "Are you thinking about marrying her?"

"Too soon to tell, sir."

Mr. Kent said, "You have a squeaky-clean record. Have a job. Why not? That would help the bureau image if you worked here."

"Just too soon, sir."

"Think you're going to fit in fine," said Mr. Kent. "You will work the evening shift. I know you were on the coffee shift at the Capitol. Don't think of it as a step down; it's a step to the next tier." Mr. Kent cocked his head and presented a quick smile. He went on, "The director of the FBI insists all employees be held to exceptional standards. Explicable conduct on and off duty must be maintained."

Mr. Kent reached into a drawer and got a voucher pad. He looked at Yoke. "Son, that Fu Manchu has to go. The director of the FBI insists all men be clean-shaven. It shows we have nothing to hide. While you're at it, get a haircut."

Keeping up an unyielding pace, he continued. "The only autonomy you will be allowed is that you will be referred to as 'Yoke,' your alias. The director doesn't want his agents confused with service employees. You will address all agents as 'mister.' Mr. Adam Ward will be your supervisor. He's from Raleigh, North Carolina, and was a member of Manley Street Congregational United Church of Christ. You probably saw him yesterday but didn't recognize him." He neglected to tell Yoke where he probably saw him. This was a tactic used to create uncertainty in targeted prospects.

Kent continued. "He went to Hampton Institute. He's a good man. I'll introduce you to him when I'm finished."

He scribbled as he filled out the voucher. "This is your allowance. Do you have a phone?"

"No, sir."

He filled in another blank and said, "Expect one by Wednesday. Pay them after the telephone technician installs it. You said you didn't drive. Have a driver's license?"

"Yes, sir."

He said as he checked a box, "Want a car?" He checked another box and said, "Nothing fancy," and detached the slip. "Take this to the cashier. Mr. Ward will escort you. Oh, I forgot." He pulled out a folder about an inch and a half thick. "Are you sure you haven't neglected to tell me anything about Stick, Kaseya, or the Queen?" He slammed the folder on the desk.

Yoke wished he could faint, but he held his ground. He said, "I've got nothing to hide."

Mr. Kent said, "If you witness Stick involved in any questionable activities, let us know. Stick's code name is 'the King.'" He put the folder in the drawer and said, "Follow me."

*   *   *

Kaseya was out for a walk on account of her sweet tooth, which craved a Butterfinger. To quash her unwarranted need, she decided to go to Rick's Convenience Store near Arkansas Avenue. As she got closer, she saw someone place a Help Wanted sign in the window. She picked up her pace and hurried inside.

A heavyset woman waited behind the register. Kaseya said, "I'm here to apply for a job."

The woman yelled, "Bobby!"

"What?" came from the back.

"This lady is here for a job," said the woman.

"Send her back."

"Go on back, honey," the woman said.

"Thanks," said Kaseya.

The back was nothing more than a storage room with a middle-aged Black man sitting behind a desk in the corner. He said as Kaseya closed in, "Glad you're interested." He stood. "What's your name?"

"Kaseya Ford."

"Well, Kaseya, why you want to work here? There are no benefits. Federal and state taxes are taken out. You'll be paid minimum wage."

"I need to make some cash to tide me over until next week."

"I see why you want to work here. You just told me you plan to work for a week. Don't be so honest. Get what you want first, then tell the rest of your story."

"Guess I blew it, huh," said Kaseya.

"You didn't blow it," said Bobby. "If you're looking for something long-term, I can help. Besides, you look too professional to be dealing with these children around here."

"What kind of a job?"

"Heard of Casino Royal over on Fourteenth and H, called the Block?" said Bobby. "They're looking for help too. You'll start out as a waitress then work your way behind the bar. Have you ever been a bartender?"

"No, but it can't be hard."

"Tell you what," he said. "See Raymond, and he'll get you started. He should be there this afternoon around six. Here." He handed her a card. "Tell 'em Bobby sent you."

*   *   *

The moment Mr. Kent stepped into the break room, the janitor's facial expressions went deadpan. The look of the spotless room made Yoke want to take his shoes off. Not one of them dared to smile. And not one of them dared to speak.

"Morning, gentlemen," said Mr. Kent. "This is Yoke. Where's Mr. Ward?"

A janitor with a Caribbean accent said, "He's on the second floor, trying to sort out a problem. He'll be back shortly."

Mr. Kent looked at a janitor who stuttered and said, "Slack, I'm going to turn him over to you. Wait here until Mr. Ward returns."

"Yes, y-yes sir," said Slack. Slack's real name was Paul Gaines Junior; he was from Hampton, South Carolina. The way he talked made people want to scream, "Give him some slack!"

Yoke sat at the table. The man with the Caribbean accent said, "I'm Quid." Mark Jacobs was from Kingston, Jamaica. He was thrifty, so those who knew him had named him after the British pound.

The rest of the janitors followed with their own introductions.

"I'm Nutty," said the short, stocky man. Newton Owens was from Newport News, Virginia. His carefree persona warranted his being called 'Nutty.'

"I'm Gimme," said a man who looked broke. Carl Robbins was from Birmingham, Alabama. He was the only janitor who had gotten his nickname from his peers. He would often order, "Gimme this" or "Gimme that."

The last man took his time looking at Yoke and said, "I'm Blue." David Bayou was from Tupelo, Mississippi. His sad eyes, which beamed from a dark-skinned face, made him look blue.

Not one of them attempted to strike up a conversation. They ignored Yoke and went back to snacking. These guys were nothing like the guys on Capitol Hill, where they moved with vigor and excitement. The guys at the FBI moved in a calculated manner. They were mindful not to cross the thin line of servitude and expendability.

A short, bug-eyed, chubby man walked in and said, "Where is he?" When he noticed the civilian clothes, he said, "I'm Mr. Ward, and you're Yoke. Welcome aboard. Slack, I'll take it from here."

Yoke stood. "Do I have to work the night ..."

"We'll get to that after I show you around," Mr. Ward said. "Stay with me."

They stepped into the corridor and traveled between occupied offices. Mr. Ward's shoulders rocked with each step of his bowed legs that struggled to support the weight of his torso. Chatter was coming from offices on both sides. When they approached two offices that stood across from each other, their doors closed, he stopped in the center of the hall.

Chatter came from behind and in front of them, but not from between these offices. Both doors were unmarked, but shadows at the bottoms of the doors revealed that they were occupied.

Mr. Ward said, "I have to be with you when you clean these rooms. Throughout this floor, the two-man concept applies. But here"—he pointed a both doors—"I have to be one of the janitors."

Yoke nodded.

"Did you get a voucher?" Mr. Ward asked.

"Yes, I did."

"Well, the funds for your voucher are taken out of these offices' accounts."

As they walked farther down the corridor, chatter grew louder. Mr. Ward said, "Try not to listen to what is being said. They don't play. Once, a janitor got into trouble; he was harassed so much, all because of what he heard. They would rather serve steak to a wino."

Yoke's stomach dropped to his balls. *This is a setup. But for what?*

"That's all you need to know for now," said Ward. "Let's go to Acquisition."

They turned the corner and walked to the cashier window. Mr. Ward asked Yoke to give her the voucher. The cashier took it, stamped it, and handed it back to him. She shuffled out $1,000 and said to Yoke, "Count it."

They left the window, and Mr. Ward said, "That money ain't for partying, not for your hooker friend, and not to pay late bills. It's to get you started. Let's go to Acquisition."

Around the corner and down the hall was Acquisition. Most of the equipment came in as evidence and was slated to be destroyed. If an agent needed something at the right time, he could get some quality equipment. In Yoke's case, it was a car.

He handed the clerk the voucher. The clerk stamped it and filed it.

The clerk went to a wall rack with car keys and picked out a set. He said, "It's the blue '65 Ford Fairlane. Fifty thousand miles, rebuilt 289, four-speed." He looked at Mr. Ward, "Sign here."

Mr. Ward scribbled and handed Yoke the keys. Yoke scribbled.

The clerk said, "It's on the second row, third car."

They went into the impound lot and inspected the Ford. Yoke looked inside and noticed a Bud Man sticker on the glove box. He said, "It'll do when you been walking for—"

"Almost four years," said Mr. Ward, "That's why your Selective Service classification is 4-F."

"My injuries in that auto accident made me unfit for military service."

"But it got you here. Let's go to Pass and ID to get your badge."

They went around the corner, and Mr. Ward said to the clerk, "He needs a badge."

The clerk said, as he looked at a roster, "Your full name?"

"Samuel Douglas Yoke."

"Oh," said the clerk, "You're Yoke. Stand against the wall next to that height chart."

Yoke stood at the wall and saw the clerk behind a Polaroid.

The clerk said, "Shoulders back and look straight ahead."

Flash.

"Got it. Wait one minute." He went to a desk and laminated the ID and put a clip on it. He then returned and said, "Here you go." He handed the badge to Yoke.

"Take the rest of the day off," Mr. Ward said. "Get a haircut and shave. You'll report tomorrow at 5:30 p.m. Your coveralls and the rest of your equipment will be in your locker. See you tomorrow."

*   *   *

It was four thirty in the afternoon when Kaseya laid a drop-waist dress on her bed. She placed a pair of six-inch heels on the floor and went to her jewelry box. She got a pearl necklace and laid it on the bed beside her dress. She turned, reached into a drawer, grabbed her undies, and went into the bathroom.

Kaseya got dressed. By now it was 5:00 p.m. She reasoned she had better get going if she was going to be on time. She grabbed a small purse, and as she got close to the door, there was a knock. She opened it, and Yoke said, "Know I should've called, but since I was in the neighborhood, thought I would drop by."

"That's sweet," she said, "but I'm in a hurry. I have some good news; I got a job. I need to be there by six."

"I'll go with you."

"You'd better walk fast."

"Not walk—I'll take you in my car," he said as he dangled his keys. She relaxed. "Thanks."

He opened the passenger door, and she got in. She tried not to make it obvious when she gave a quick inspection of the interior.

He said as he got in, "Since you're the first passenger, I'll call it the Bud Man Special."

They made their way to Fourteenth and cruised.

"How did it go?" she asked.

"On the surface, everything is good," he said, "Going to be working at the FBI building."

She said, "Wow, that's great. By the way things look, you got a raise too."

"In a way," he said, "I did. They gave me a car and a grand to start. Get this: I get a phone Wednesday."

"You're truly blessed. I'll be working at the Casino Royal. It's funny how we're blessed on the same day."

"Hope so, but it's still strange," he said as he parked along Fourteenth on the side of the club at 5:50 p.m.

They went inside, and Kaseya said to a bartender, "Here to see Raymond; Bobby sent me."

Raymond, a Jewish man with flair, walked by the bar and said as he got closer, "Kaseya, you look great!"

He held her hand and said, "Thanks, Yoke, for bringing her. Have a drink on us at the bar while I discuss the job with Kaseya." He led her to the back.

It was 8:30 p.m. when Yoke and Kaseya left a barbecue café and headed back to her apartment. Yoke said, "Thought it was strange he knew my name."

"I did too," she replied. "Probably nothing. I'll be working from six to closing."

"What a coincidence. I'm on the night shift. That means I can drop you off and pick you up."

"Things are really working out."

"I'm not a holy roller," said Yoke, "but going to church with you—I think it changed things." He retrieved his crucifix and kissed it.

CHAPTER 4

Tuesday morning, Yoke's first stop was the barbershop.

Mr. Edwards, a barber, called out, "Next!"

Yoke went and sat in his chair. He said to Mr. Edwards, "Number two with a shave."

Stick walked in and exclaimed, "The king is here!"

One barber said, "Ready for the Seventy-Sixers?"

"Gone wear them out," said Stick.

Another barber said, "Dream on, rookie."

"Forget you, man," said Stick. "What's happening, Yoke? How did it go yesterday?"

"Like diarrhea. Steady flow, but it still stinks."

"See, you were overreacting," said Stick. "Didn't I tell you that?"

"You were right."

Stick said as he whirled around, "Bring all your troubles to the king, and I'll ease your burdens."

Another barber said scornfully, "Nigga, please."

One barber said as he read the newspaper, "The garbage men talking about striking in Memphis."

Stick sat in a waiting chair and asked, "Yoke, what's it like at the FBI?"

"Don't know. Yesterday was my first day."

"Bet you can't drink, smoke, party, or even screw, right?"

A barber said, "Those FBI agents are some boring cats."

Another barber said, "Shut up, fool. Don't want them snooping around here. Stick, let's talk about something else."

When Mr. Edwards was finished, Yoke waited until another barber finished Stick's haircut. When they walked outside, Stick started walking down Fourteenth, but Yoke stood by his car with a smile.

Stick turned around and said, "Come on, man."

"Okay," Yoke replied, "you walk, I drive."

"What? You got a car?"

"Yep," said Yoke, "got it yesterday. Don't just stand there; get in." Stick got in, and they rode off.

"Damn, you kept your job, and they gave you a raise. You're a bad man," said Stick "Tell you what I'm going to do with my first paycheck. We're going to put on a tux and hit Casino Royal."

"That'll be cool. Kaseya works there."

"Not for long," Stick said. "I'm going to pay for y'all wedding, and I'll hire you."

"What's my job?"

"Cleaning up my mansion, fool."

Yoke parked on Fourteenth Street in the business district. They got out and stood outside Cavaliers. Yoke said, "I'm still a little worried."

"Guess you have to be there a while before that goes away. Just like basketball. When you play before a big crowd, you think all eyes are on you. But when you think about it, eyes are scattered on all ten players on the court. The only time they think about you is when you get the ball. That's when you show your stuff."

"That's what I learned yesterday, and that's why I'm worried. Sometimes eyes are on you, and you don't know it. Somebody's always watching."

"Well, keep on worrying," said Stick. "I'm going to keep on moving ahead."

* * *

Kaseya sat in a chair while Melba was sprawled on the sofa. As they watched the soaps, Kaseya said, "You never told me what the Queen said."

"Nothing," said Melba.

"I think Yoke is pretty cool. Things seems to always work out for him."

"That square is lucky," said Melba. "You two are made for each other. A square peg for a square hole."

"Bump you. Listen, I'll talk to Yoke and see if he'll drop you off at Club Mare."

"He'll have to drop me off two blocks up," said Melba. "Don't want no FBI checking me out."

"Okay, Paranoid Patty. How are you and Stick getting along?"

"He's my regular customer," said Melba as she sat up. "Don't think he wants a relationship. He likes fooling around. That guy keeps a bankroll. He's fit for the pros. He doesn't have to look forward to paydays. Paydays find him."

"Are you sure he's on the up?"

"Betcha he doesn't worry," said Melba. "He has so much confidence, he makes luck say, 'Screw it.'"

* * *

That afternoon at 5:20, Yoke walked down the corridor to the custodian room. As he passed one of the closed-door offices, an agent came out, and Yoke heard, "T. O. Jones."

Yoke went into the custodian room, and the moment he stepped in, the janitors clammed up. "Where's my locker?" Yoke asked.

Quid tapped the locker next to him. "Here, mon."

Yoke opened it, examined the contents, and said, "Where's my lock?"

Nutty, a light-skinned man of average build, said, "We don't need 'em."

Their demeanor reflected the culture of the FBI. Honesty, integrity, and faith all rolled into a small job that only mattered to them. Outside that room, they were looked upon with suspicion.

As Yoke put on his coveralls, Mr. Ward looked in and said, "Yoke, we'll clean the closed-door offices. Grab that trash can and put it on a dolly."

"Yes sir," said Yoke.

"Slack," said Mr. Ward, "You're coming with me and Yoke. Grab that hand truck."

"Y-yes, yes sir," said Slack.

"Nutty, you'll buff the halls with Quid. Gimme and Blue, y'all know what to do. Let's go to work."

Yoke and Slack followed Mr. Ward to the first closed-door office on the right. Mr. Ward said to Yoke, "Leave the trash can out here and follow us." He unlocked the door, and they stepped in. Inside the office, the desks were naked, and the walls were covered. There were no trash cans at the desk. A teleprinter was in the back. Next to the door were office paper boxes stacked four feet high. Slack slid the hand truck under the boxes and wheeled them out.

"Let's go across the hall," Mr. Ward said. He unlocked the door. "Bring that trash can in here."

Yoke pulled the can inside an office with two rows of empty desks. Beside each of the desks was a wastebasket. There was a Siemens T100 telex machine at the front. The next room over had a Plexiglas wall that revealed a switchboard for two operators. Outside the door was a wastebasket. Unlike the other office, the walls weren't covered in this one. Posted on the walls were candid photos of Black Americans. Yoke recognized a person in one photo. It was Stick. Under his photograph was a card with "King" written on it.

Mr. Ward said, "Hurry up. The quicker we go, the better."

Yoke dumped each wastebasket with urgency. After all the baskets were emptied, Yoke pushed the trash can into the hall. Mr. Ward locked the door, and they followed him to an elevator. They then went down to the burn room. There they emptied the trash can into the furnace. The office boxes required two people to toss them into the furnace. After they were finished, they went up in the elevator. "Slack," Mr. Ward said, "find Quid so he can show Yoke the ropes."

"Yes, y-yes sir."

*   *   *

Over on H Street NW, people left the speakeasy on the first floor and made their way up to Casino Royal. Inside the six-hundred-seat club, Marvin Gaye's "Too Busy Thinking About My Baby" played over laughter and chatter.

Kaseya waited on customers with Yoke on her mind. She jotted down a table order and took it to the bar.

Raymond said over the music, "You really know what you're doing."

"Doing my best," she replied, and she called out the drink orders to the bartender. Her orders were filled, and she returned to the table.

One fellow said, "My, you're proficient."

"Thank you, sir. Do you request a tab?"

"Naw, honey," he said, and he paid her.

She went back to the bar, paid the bartender, and returned to the floor. Bee Gees' "Bridges Crossing Rivers" played as she browsed. She walked past a table and overheard two Black men deep in conversation.

One man said, "Garbage men talking about a strike."

The other man said, "Shame the way those men died."

She strolled on, and in no time, she was waiting on three tables at a time. Maybe it was her outfit. Maybe it was her sexy demeanor. In either case, she was glad to be working. Now she believed she had something to offer Yoke. She pranced from table to table as James Brown's "Say It Loud—I'm Black and I'm Proud" played.

*　　*　　*

It was 10:15 p.m. at the FBI Headquarters. Yoke sat with the others at the table on their lunch break. Again, he was surrounded by deadpan faces. It was as though their tongues were being held hostage.

Even when they spoke, they said little of note.

"How was your day?" asked Blue.

Gimme said, "Watched television and went to the store."

Their conversations were bland and offered only general information. Not one of them asked Yoke about anything. They didn't even look his way.

At eleven, lunch was over. Yoke pushed away from the table and headed for the door. Pandemonium broke out.

The others yelled, "Wait, man, wait!"

Quid said, "We got to leave together." He smiled and walked out with Yoke.

*　　*　　*

At 2:30 a.m. on Wednesday, Yoke pulled up to the block of Fourteenth and H. Kaseya was the best thing he had seen all night. An overcoat concealed her provocative outfit as she stepped to the car.

She said as she got in, "How was your day?"

"Crazy," he said. "Don't know how to read those guys."

"My night was fabulous. That job is so easy. Look." She flashed a wad. "Payday? I'm in the moola, baby."

He smiled as he drove on Fourteenth and said, "Best news I've heard all day. Wonder what the rest of today will bring?"

CHAPTER 5

Later that morning, a knock came at Yoke's door. "Who is it?" he answered.

A husky voice replied, "Bell Telephone service."

Yoke opened the door, and the telephone man said with an outstretched clipboard, "Sign here."

He scribbled his signature, and the telephone man went to work. After the phone was installed, the man said, "Here's your number. If you have any problems, let us know."

"How much?" asked Yoke.

"It'll be on your first bill." With that, the man closed his equipment box and left.

* * *

In the office at Howard University's men's dormitory, a student answered the phone, got up, and went to Stick's room.

"Stick, telephone."

Stick followed him to the office and answered, "Yeah, what?"

"This Yoke. Got my phone. Here's my number."

"Wait." He grabbed a pen and paper. "Mop the floor... Just kidding; I'm ready." He wrote down the number. "That's cool. Now I don't have to walk to get you to do something for me."

"Okay, whatcha need?"

Stick said, "Need you to take me downtown to meet my scout."

"When?"

"Now, man." Stick hung up.

*   *   *

Yoke waited outside the dorm. Stick walked to the car with bouncing steps. After he got in, he said, "Let's go to the strip."

"What will you do if you don't make the pros?" Yoke asked.

Stick looked at Yoke disappointedly and said, "Look, doubting Thomas, no confidence ain't good."

"I'm just saying. What if your plans fall through?"

"I don't have to worry about that. Pull over here and I'll show you." He got out and walked to a White man.

The man's hat shielded his eyes, but his smile was easy to see. When he reached into his windbreaker and pulled out an envelope, Yoke looked across the street at a Safeway on the corner. He watched a man who appeared to be experiencing hard times stroll inside.

Stick got back in the car and said, "See?"

Yoke said firmly, "Don't want to talk about it!"

"You asked me," said Stick.

"Don't wanna talk about it. Let's get something to eat."

*   *   *

At the same time, at FBI Headquarters, Mr. Kent called Mr. Ward. "Got some hard news. You're going to be one down this afternoon."

"You mean I'm going to be short again?" said Ward.

"That's right. We don't have any control over it. The director only wants reliable people."

"Well," said Ward, "I'll try to make some adjustments, but I can't guarantee quality."

"Do your best. Soon as Yoke comes in, send him to me."

"Will do." He hung up. "Damn."

*   *   *

Kaseya was up and about in her apartment. Melba came in and went straight to the fridge. She poured a glass of milk and sat at the dinette table.

"You look rough," Kaseya said. "Where you been?"

"Stayed at the Park Road Hotel last night," said Melba. "Damn, he wore me out."

"Who? Stick?"

"Naw, some other guy I know."

"Slow down, Nelly; you got a lot more plowing to do."

"So when are you going to start? Yoke's a man, and men don't wait too long. He'll move on, and he won't even tell you. You'll hear it from a friend like me."

"He ain't going nowhere. Our thing is coming together. He won't blow it."

Melba said, "You mean you're going to work at the casino forever?" She folded her arms, looked away, and said, "Don't think so."

"What's wrong with that?" said Kaseya, "His work schedule is the same as mine. Besides, we're going shopping before we go to work."

"Shopping for what? You mean you lost the key to your chastity belt."

"Thanks for reminding me. While we're out, we'll stop at People's Drug Store and pick up some condoms"—Kaseya looked at Melba—"for you."

"Don't worry about me," said Melba. "This boat doesn't have any holes."

"Screw you," said Kaseya, "I've got to get dressed." She went to her bedroom.

There was a knock at the door. Melba got up and opened it, and Yoke walked in. "See Stick last night?" he asked.

"Naw," she said. "He didn't stop at the club."

Kaseya came into the room and said, "Let's go." She grabbed her purse. "Need to be back by four."

Yoke handed Kaseya a slip of paper. "Here's my phone number."

"Cool," she said, and she led him out the door.

When Yoke started the car, Sam Cooke was crooning "A Change Is Gonna Come" over the radio.

Kaseya said, "You got that right. Take me to Fodor's." They headed to the U Street corridor.

"Feels like cloud nine," said Yoke, "Got you. Got a phone and money in my pocket. It's all cool."

"I feel good too. I believe you're serious."

"You Can't Lose What You Ain't Never Had" by Muddy Waters played.

"We're getting there," said Yoke. "Can't say it's a sure thing. You'll meet a lot of guys at the club."

"Don't worry about me. You watch yourself, okay?"

"Sure," he said, "That's a sure thing."

Inside Fodor's fashion shop, "High Hopes," sung with Sinatra's flair, filled the boutique. As she browsed through the skirts, she said,

"Need to go to Bargintown when we leave here. Got to pick up some things for the apartment."

"No problem. Going to stop at Garfinkel's to get a hat," Yoke said. "You know, we get along fine." He held her. "After being with you all day, what could go wrong?"

* * *

Yoke stood before Mr. Kent, who was seated at his desk. "On strike ..." came over the intercom. "Thank you," said Mr. Kent. He gave the impression of a man who looked busy, but he wasn't. Mr. Kent knew the contents in the folder on his desk. He studied the documents and then closed the folder.

Yoke knew they never asked questions they didn't know the answers to. He thought, *Okay, let's have it.*

Mr. Kent said, "What happened this morning with King?"

"Nothing, Mr. Kent."

"You screwed up," Kent said rudely. "Did you see Stick King receive any money from his scout?"

Yoke answered honestly. "No, I didn't. If I had, I would've called."

"Don't play games with me, son," said Kent. "You didn't see him get money because you looked away."

Yoke said, "A man caught my attention at Safeway. That's what I saw."

"What you *didn't* see," said Kent. "King took money from a scout who works for the Justice Department. If you had witnessed the transfer, we could've nailed King." It was a misdirection tactic. He wanted Yoke to witness the benefits of working at the bureau.

Yoke said with confidence, "That's entrapment, sir."

Mr. Kent stood behind his desk and said with fury, "Don't lecture me about my job. You watermelon mother ..." He caught himself, regained his composure, and proceeded. "You're just a janitor. Don't tell me how to do my job, and I won't try to learn yours. Now get out of my office and tell Quid to come and see me."

Mr. Ward was waiting outside the door. When Yoke stepped out, he went in, and before he closed the door, Mr. Ward pleaded, "Don't do it. He likes it here." The door closed.

*   *   *

At the same time, in the break room, Slack said, "At first, I I-I thought he was a plant."

"Me too," said Gimme.

"Slack Don't believe he was," said Blue.

"Feel the same way, Blue," Quid replied. "But mon, he was strange."

"He wasn't strange," Nutty said. "It's the way we treated him, giving him the cold shoulder."

*   *   *

Yoke turned from Kent's office and left. He walked past the closed-door offices and saw that the doors were open. The agents were busy—all chatter with no laughter. As he walked down the hall, he didn't know how he was going to tell Kaseya. He felt he'd probably lose her too. He thought about the car and phone. He would probably have to give them up. There was a chance he could keep the money and use it to tide him over, but they would probably want that too. He walked into the break room and said on his way to his locker, "Quid, Mr. Kent wants to see you."

Anxiety struck Slack, Gimme, Nutty, and Blue. They sat back. Gimme lit a cigarette. Blue started humming, and Nutty kept his eyes on Yoke.

Yoke gathered his personal items from his locker and closed it.

Gimme said with a cigarette trembling between his fingers, "Where're you going?"

"Got fired," said Yoke.

Blue said, "Must've screwed up bad."

"I did," he said. "Didn't want to bust a friend."

"Was it either you or him?" Nutty asked.

"Yeah," said Yoke. "Don't want to play no more." He headed for the door, but Mr. Ward looked in.

Mr. Ward said to Yoke, "Where're you going?"

"Home, sir," said Yoke.

"No you're not. You going to work with Slack tonight." He looked at the rest of the janitors. "Gimme, Nutty, and Blue, y'all work together as a team. Let's go to work."

Yoke dropped a ton of anxiety on his way back to his locker.

* * *

It was jazz night at the Casino Royal. The free-bop style of Miles Davis was entrenched in his composition "I Thought of You." Kaseya waited at the bar, watching tables.

Raymond said, "Kind of slow, but things will pick up. Save your energy for later."

"Okay," she replied.

Two men sat at the bar. One man said to another, "Don't take much to set them off."

The other man said, "Right, but you got to understand the way they feel. If those men were White, it wouldn't take much to send somebody to prison."

"It'll die down by the end of the week."

A table of four waved Kaseya over. The piano keys danced as she made her way. While she took the orders, the Ramsey Lewis Trio pinged and thumped "The In Crowd."

*   *   *

At 10:00 p.m., the janitors entered the break room. The first thing to catch their eyes was that Quid's locker had been cleared out with the door left open. Yoke looked at the other janitors, and they looked at him.

Mr. Ward came in and said, "Quid won't be back anytime soon. Get used to it until I get a replacement. Tried to save him, but the order was above my pay grade."

Yoke sat at the table and opened his brown paper bag. Gimme, Nutty, and Blue sat on one side. Slack sat beside Yoke. They ate, and when they were finished, they went back to work. Yoke noticed that the last man to leave the closed-door office carried a travel bag. He thought, *Overtime.* No wonder they didn't have to tidy up that room.

*   *   *

Yoke picked up Kaseya at 2:30 a.m. As they traveled on Fourteenth, he said, "I feel like a screwup. On Capitol Hill, I could do no wrong. At the FBI, I can't do anything right."

Sam and Dave's "Hold On, I'm Comin'" played on the radio.

"That's the way it goes," Kaseya said, "Sometimes you're up; sometimes you're down. That's just life."

"That's the most stressful job I've ever worked," Yoke replied. "Everybody in that building is so uptight. Tension is the normal atmosphere. Don't see how they like it. They've worked there so long; guess they're used to it."

"Tired of seeing you uptight."

He pulled in front of her apartments and parked.

"Come on," she said. The moment she opened the door, she added, "Go to my bedroom."

"What?"

"Just go," she said, and she took off her coat. She followed him into the bedroom. He stood at the side of the bed. "Get in bed. Whether we fall asleep in each other's arms or make love, in either case, something's going to happen tonight."

CHAPTER 6

Stick called Yoke, but there was no answer. So he called his scout, Jake.

"What's going on?" Jake asked.

Stick said, "A guy has been following me the last couple of days. Last night I didn't set foot off campus."

"He's probably an obsessed fan," said Jake. "Get used to it. At least he's not bad as the reporters."

"No worry here. I can take him. What gets me is he shows no fear. He knows I know he's watching me."

"Okay, don't get bent out of shape," said Jake. "I'll put some detectives on him."

"Cool," said Stick.

* * *

Kaseya stayed wrapped in Yoke's arms at noon. Both were nude, and both acted as if it was nothing. They accepted the night for what it was—just another night. As they got dressed, not a word was spoken until she said, "Bacon or sausage?"

"Bacon," he said.

"How do you want your eggs?"

"Scrambled."

As she separated bacon strips in a skillet, she asked, "Was it wrong?"

"No," he said. "It's me. You made me feel alive again. But I'm afraid. All this week, every time I felt good, something bad happened. I want to shout for joy." He kissed his crucifix and went on. "All I do is pray. Kaseya, I want you. Don't want to lose you."

"You worry when you shouldn't," she said. "Don't want to lose you either."

"What are we going to do?" said Yoke.

She said as she scrambled the eggs, "Take it slow. Last night, we needed that. We have the rest of our lives to fall in love."

"You're a miracle," he said.

"Not a miracle. I care for you." She fixed his plate and put it before him. She got the toast from the oven and gave him a slice. She got her plate and sat down, and while Yoke blessed the food, the phone rang.

Kaseya got up and answered. "Hi Stick. No, she's not here, but your homeboy is—Yoke." She handed him the phone.

"What's up?" Yoke asked.

"How about taking me to Sears," said Stick.

"Okay, let me finish eating. I'll pick you up at the dorm." He hung up.

*　*　*

Stick got into the car and said, "Somebody been following me."

"I would too," said Yoke. "If every day is payday, somebody bound to know. The ghetto wire is hot."

"Why me? I can take him, and he knows it. It's like he wants to harass me."

"What does he look like?"

"Average height. Average build. Looks like a loser."

Yoke had seen him at Safeway. After putting things together, he believed the guy was FBI. He couldn't discuss it with Stick, so he said, "No matter what problems he has, he better not put his hands on you."

"Thanks, man," said Stick. "Tonight, can you pick up Melba and take her to work?"

"If she needs a ride, right on."

"I called you this morning, and you didn't answer. I called Melba; you were there with Kaseya. Did you spend the night?"

There was no way he was going to let Stick know what happened. "Went over to her apartment early this morning." Yoke parked at Sears. "Hurry up. Oh, and another thing. Never conduct your business in front of me again."

"Hold your horses," said Stick. "From now on, I won't."

* * *

On the way back to the dorm, Stick said, "That's him."

"Where?" asked Yoke.

Stick pointed. "In front of Safeway."

Yoke wanted to keep driving. All he needed was something to give Mr. Kent to talk about. "Let's go in the store. Need to buy some gum." He pulled over and parked.

The moment Stick got out; the hard-case man stared him down. Yoke walked ahead as Stick returned the look intently. By then Yoke had walked past the man. He went to the door and waited.

The man stepped behind Yoke and stood in front of Stick. The man said to Stick, "You think you're slick."

"If you don't get out my face," said Stick, "I'll slap you back to Africa!"

The man said, "We know you got Whitey's protection. You're big in Black colleges but wait and you'll see; those boys from those big universities are gonna school ya."

"What's your point? Why are you following me?"

"You go to Howard, so you're not stupid. You know why. Just like Mr. Edwards in the barbershop. We got our eyes on him too."

Mr. Edwards owned the barbershop across from Safeway and was Yoke's barber. He was the one who had who turned Stick onto Jake the year before. Neighborhood gossip indicated Mr. Edwards was into something heavy. Every now and then, White men went into his shop, although there were no barbers in the shop known to have enough experience to cut their hair.

Yoke said to the man, "Leave Mr. Edwards alone. Come on, Stick."

The man said to Yoke, "One day you're gonna realize you're a snake charmer." He looked at Stick and said, "Snake!"

Stick walked around him and went into the store.

Yoke figured he was going to catch hell from Mr. Kent. If he lost his job over that encounter, he didn't need the job in the first place. Besides, he was confident Mr. Smith would hire him back.

*   *   *

Kaseya said to Melba, "What's up with you and Stick?"

"Nothing, just friends," said Melba.

"Right. He's getting ready for the pros, and you still hang on to that gig."

"Sometimes you must go with the flow," said Melba. "He's going to meet a lot of women in Philadelphia. He'll probably meet doctors, lawyers, and professional women. Why build on hope?"

"What if he wants you to be the mother of his children. Don't need a profession for that."

Melba giggled. "You're so naive. Rich women have babies too. The difference is their children are planned, so it's not an inconvenience. Stick is going to be on the road more than the average pencil pusher. Government pencil pushers keep my purse fat. Stick can take me or leave me. Either way, I'll be all right."

"Don't you have feelings?" Kaseya asked.

"Feelings are for chumps." Melba looked Kaseya in the eye. "Nobody promised you a great life. Not even your folks. Why develop feelings for someone you don't know? That's foolish."

"Life isn't a hustle. It's real. Yoke came along, and I feel there's something there. He cares for me, and I care for him. That's not weak; that's living without fear."

"I'm supposed to meet Stick tonight," said Melba, "Let's sit around and talk about them after Yoke bring us home."

"Bet."

*   *   *

That afternoon, after Yoke dropped Kaseya and Melba off, he was walking down the corridor when Mr. Ward stepped out of Mr. Kent's office. Yoke knew what had occurred and was ready to own up to it.

Mr. Ward said, "Boy, what did you do?"

"I know," Yoke said resignedly. "Mr. Kent wants to see me."

"No," said Mr. Ward. "He thinks you're perfect. He likes the way you fell in place at the right time. Go on to the break room."

Yoke was confused. One minute he was wrong; the next minute he was right. He thought, *Screw it, just another day.*

In the break room, the fellows were sitting at the table. Yoke took a seat next to Blue. Mr. Ward came in, followed by a young White man.

Mr. Ward said to them, "This is Squirrel from the coffee crew upstairs." The coffee crew was named from all the cleanup spills during the day. Pony "Squirrel" Reese was an outdoorsman and a rock 'n' roll artist.

Mr. Ward said, "He's from Blytheville, Arkansas."

Yoke found himself like the others. He remained silent. That guy probably is a plant. He was picked to watch them and report back to Kent. It was at that moment that Yoke began to understand why Blue, Slack, Gimme, and Nutty treated him coldly.

Mr. Ward said to Squirrel, "Grab that trash can and put it on a dolly. Blue, grab the hand truck. Yoke, you, and Slack will do the halls. Blue and Gimme, y'all know what to do."

Yoke tapped on the locker and said to Squirrel, "This yours."

*   *   *

In the hall, Slack poured wax ahead of Yoke while he mopped from side to side.

Slack said, "I-I'm scared. That's two, t-two guys gone. Don't know why, w-why."

"Don't know either," said Yoke. "Wonder what Quid did? Thought he was cool."

Slack said, "H-he, he was. That Mr. Ward is a sneaky man. He, he doesn't tell us nothing."

"He's not supposed to tell," said Yoke. "The way he treated Squirrel was the same way he treated me."

"M-me, me too."

*   *   *

At 2:45 a.m., Yoke and Kaseya went to Club Madre. He parked and said to Kaseya, "Things are coming too fast at me."

"What's wrong?" she asked.

"Nothing. We got another guy today, and they treated him the same way they treated me. Don't know what to think."

Stick and Melba came out hugging. Yoke noticed the hard-case man with two heavies.

The hard-case man yelled at Stick, "Be glad when you're in Philly."

Stick released Melba and said, "Don't know you, man, but you're starting to piss me off."

"There's two ways to do this. Get cut from the Sixers or get cut by my razor rat now."

Yoke jumped out of the car and said to the man, "Mind your business. Let's go, Stick."

"Oh," said the man, "You want some too?"

He swung the razor back and forth at Stick and then sliced at Yoke. In the follow-through, Yoke caught the man's arm and twisted his wrist. The razor plummeted to the pavement. Stick punched one man and backhanded the other. Spectators watched as bodies rumbled fiercely on the sidewalk. Ten fists were thrown from all directions and landed with ruthless intentions.

By now a crowd had formed. Metro detectives arrived on the scene, forced their way through, and separated the tussling men.

One detective shouted at Yoke and Stick, "Want you out of here now!"

As Yoke climbed into the car, Stick said, "See what I mean? Can't have any fun."

"You asked for that life," said Yoke. But in Yoke's mind, he knew he had messed up again. FBI employees aren't supposed to get into trouble at speakeasy clubs.

* * *

Friday morning at FBI Headquarters, an agent from upstairs handed Mr. Kent a memo. It read,

The program's goal is to prevent the coalition of militant black nationalist groups to prevent the Rise of a 'messiah' who could unify the militant black nationalist movement ... To prevent black nationalist groups and leaders from gaining respectability, by discrediting them ... especially among youth ... figures with the necessary charisma to be a real threat for a much more militant vision of black power.

Mr. Kent's program was well in tune with the memo, in that intelligence was firing on all cylinders.

*   *   *

That afternoon, Yoke took his time on his way to work. Why hurry to get fired? He had screwed up and couldn't come up with a believable excuse. What made things worse was that he had been with Stick. Yet he refused to feel guilty for helping his friend. In fact, he felt good knowing his girl had watched him as he fought. He relented in thought. *Maybe cleaning Stick's mansion isn't a bad idea.*

On the way to the break room, he saw Mr. Ward sway out of Kent's office. Mr. Ward waved at Yoke and rocked from side to side to the break room. Just as Yoke entered, Mr. Ward said, "Slack, Mr. Kent wants to see you."

Slack spilled his milk. Blue, Gimme, and Nutty looked at Yoke. Squirrel looked impassive. Slack got up and walked as though he were headed for death row. He paused in front of Yoke and said, "You, y-you of all people," and he walked out.

Mr. Ward said, "Gimme, you, Blue, and Yoke do the offices. Nutty and Squirrel, do the floors."

"Thought you had to be with us," Yoke said.

Mr. Ward handed him the keys and said, "Mr. Kent approved you to act on my behalf. Fill you in after lunch."

Yoke worried. Was Mr. Ward's job on the chopping block? *Quid and now Slack gone, why? Maybe Mr. Kent didn't get the word about last night. When Mr. Kent finds out, all hell is going to break loose.* He needed to be cool and not mention it to Mr. Ward.

Yoke unlocked the door. Gimme and Blue put the office paper boxes on the hand truck. Blue wheeled it out. Yoke stepped across the hall and opened the other office. He stepped in and noticed a candid photograph of the hard-case man next to Stick's photograph. Gimme and Blue emptied the wastebaskets. Yoke kept an eye on the teleprinter. Nothing came over the line. After they were finished, they went straight to the burn room. Not one word was spoken.

*   *   *

After lunch, Mr. Ward approached Yoke, headed for the door. He said to Yoke, "Give me the keys."

He handed the keys over and said, "Everything went without any problems."

"I know," Mr. Ward replied. "Mr. Kent heard about last night."

Yoke looked down and remained silent.

"Mr. Kent said you did the right thing. They're not ready to bust Stick. They need him to lead them to other players."

"Thought the bureau were going to blame you," said Yoke, "but what happened to Quid and Slack is none of my business."

"You're right," said Mr. Ward. "Keep it that way. There're two words you need to remember. The first word is 'discrediting' and, you did that last night. Those three men are going to spend thirty days in jail."

As they strolled out of the break room Yoke said, "But they have to go to court."

"Doesn't matter. It's coming down the pipe."

"What's the second word?"

"'Disrupt,'" said Ward. "You'll discover that soon."

"If that's all, have a good weekend."

"You too," said Mr. Ward.

Still, something didn't sit right with Yoke. He believed Mr. Ward was holding back.

* * *

Saturday morning, Yoke went to the gym and saw Stick as he sat on the bleachers. He dropped beside Stick and said, "How you feel?"

"No worries. Just the usual hassles. The good news ... I'm supposed to meet my agent tomorrow."

Yoke thought for a second and said, "Are you finished with Jake?"

"He's still in the picture. My agent is just another sure thing."

"Cool. Let's hang out at Casino Royal tonight. We can pick up Melba at Club Madre."

"Sounds like a winner," Stick said. He then yelled, "We got next."

* * *

After Yoke was finished at the gym, he went to check on his mother. He knew she would be waiting eagerly, and when he pulled up to her row house, he saw her in the window with her hands on her jaw. She hustled from the window. Her door was open before he knocked.

"Boy," she said, "what's that you got there?"

"It's my car." He handed her a piece of paper. "And here's my telephone number."

She took the paper. "God has really blessed you. How about taking me to the grocery store."

"Okay, Ma," he said. "I'll wait."

She left the living room to get dressed.

*   *   *

That night Kaseya was busy as The Impressions' "We're a Winner" rippled throughout the club. The patrons' dress code had businessmen in dark suits and women in evening dresses. Booze flowed freely while chatter competed with music. Yoke walked into the club dressed in Capitol Hill fashion: a suit and tie with wing tips. He was tailed by Stick, who was in a flashy pinstripe suit with dress boots. Kaseya was there to take their order the moment they sat at a table.

"Hurry and give me your order," she said. "That table over there has been waiting."

"Anything wet," said Yoke.

Stick replied, "Crown on the rocks."

She made a mental note and went to another table.

"Why do you keep Melba hanging on?" Yoke asked.

"She knows the deal," said Stick. "She dates other guys to make me jealous."

"Don't get it," said Yoke. "You approached her. She took the bait, and now you're dragging her along. Have some guts. Let her know how you really feel."

Stick said, "Ain't seen half the women I'm going to see when I'm pro."

"That's your problem," said Yoke, "All they want is your money. At least Melba is with you on your way up."

"Lady Madonna" resounded throughout the club as Stick said, "Easy to say, brother. When are you going to tap Kaseya?" He paused. "Huh? Cat got your tongue?"

Yoke still neglected to tell him what had happened the other night. He said, "Don't think she looks at me like that."

"Bull," said Stick. "I'm not blind. I see the way she looks at you. If you sneeze, her panties will drop to the floor."

"Naw, man, you got it all wrong," said Yoke. "Remember: she didn't give into that White guy, and that got her fired."

"Bet if you beg, she'll give in," said Stick. "I feel bad because I'm getting laid left and right, and my homeboy isn't."

Yoke said at the introduction to Sly and the Family Stone's "Dance to the Music," "Enough, here come our drinks."

*   *   *

At 2:30 a.m., they entered the living room at the ladies' apartment. Kaseya searched the radio dial for a jazz station. Melba followed Stick to a chair and sat in his lap. When the radio reception was clear, Kaseya joined Yoke on the sofa.

Stick said, "Moms wants me to come home soon. I can hitch a ride with some students that's going on a field trip."

"Good," said Yoke, "a well-deserved rest. Need you out of my hair."

"So, before I go, why don't you let Dr. Stick King fix your relationship?"

Kaseya laughed. "You? When you and Melba really hook up and stop playing the dating game, we'll listen to you."

"Turning down professional help," said Stick. "Can't understand it." He yawned. "Feeling a little sleepy. Let's go, Melba."

She giggled. "Okay." She then stood and went to her bedroom.

"Time for me to go," Yoke said.

"How I'm going to get to the dorm?" asked Stick.

"Call me, fool."

Kaseya walked Yoke to the door and said, "Thanks for everything. Call me tomorrow?"

"All right," he said, and they kissed.

Yoke left with the impression that she knew how to push his buttons. However, it wasn't enough for him to let his guard down. And being on Mr. Kent's good side didn't sit right with him.

CHAPTER 7

The following Monday afternoon, Yoke arrived early for work. He noticed the closed-door offices had been left open and were empty. He went to the break room and put on his coveralls.

Gimme and Blue walked in and went straight to their lockers. They were followed by Nutty. Then Squirrel came in with an electric guitar. He placed the guitar in his locker and grabbed his coveralls.

Gimme said to Squirrel as he sat at the table, "How was your weekend?"

The others waited to hear his response. They were curious to see would he run off at the mouth or just give the usual general answer.

Squirrel took the bait. "Our concert went great," he said.

"What kind of music y'all play?" Blue asked.

Squirrel said as he fastened his coveralls, "We play rock."

"What do y'all call yourselves?"

"Dead Puppies."

The room broke into hysterical laughter. Nutty asked, "How did y'all come up with that?"

"President Kennedy's brother Joseph was killed in World War Two," said Squirrel. "Kennedy was assassinated five years ago. They died in their prime. Our group is a tribute to them."

"Your brand of philosophy jams with those far-out lyrics," said Yoke. "Bet you can make that guitar scream."

"I do," Squirrel said. "That's what our fans pay to hear—my solos."

"The world is full of nuts," Nutty said, "But I think you're going to be our new overseer. Since you're White."

"Nope," said Squirrel, "I gig like you."

Mr. Ward moved from side to side into the break room and said, "This is Pearl from East St. Louis. His real name was William Jones. He was considered the gem of East Saint Louis. Introduce yourself to him later. For now, the offices are empty. The analysts had a meeting upstairs. When they're finished, they're going home."

Yoke didn't want to be responsible for the keys. It looked like a trap. He said, "What're our assignments since the offices are opened?"

"You and Nutty will do the floors," said Mr. Ward. "Gimme, grab the hand truck. Pearl, get that tall trash can and put it on a dolly. We'll do the closed-door offices. Blue and Squirrel, y'all do the general offices. Let's go to work."

Nutty dry-mopped the hall, leaving a curvy pattern. It was a dead giveaway that he was nervous. Ordinarily, the pattern was straight so that the polish would always land on a swept floor. Yoke asked, "What's wrong? You're missing parts of the floor."

"Can't groove today," Nutty said. He didn't want Yoke to know that the remaining janitors believed that the one who worked with Yoke would be the next one to leave.

*   *   *

At lunch, the squeaky sound of an electric guitar filled the break room. Squirrel strummed the strings with precision without the aid of an amplifier. In between chords, he would take bites from his sandwich.

"No wonder they sent you down here," Gimme said.

"Yeah, it's our turn to suffer," Blue responded.

"I'm with Blue," Pear stated. "Mississippi blues is the joint."

Yoke said to Pearl, "I'm Yoke from right here in DC. How long have you been here?"

"For a while," Pearl replied.

Yoke, Gimme, and Blue relaxed knowing he wasn't a blabbermouth. Nutty didn't show any emotion. He was preoccupied with the thought that he was next. Squirrel remained impassive. After lunch, they finished their details.

When they returned to the break room, a note had been posted: REPORT TOMORROW AT 7:00 p.m.

Gimme asked Mr. Ward, "Will we have to work to 3:00 a.m.?"

"No," said Mr. Ward. "Some of the analysts will be working late."

Mr. Ward said to Yoke as he took off his coveralls, "You're going to have Wednesday off. Plan accordingly."

"Why?" asked Yoke.

"Don't ask why; just do it, fool."

*　*　*

At 2:15 a.m. on Tuesday, Yoke picked up Kaseya. On the way to her apartment, he said, "Got Wednesday off."

"Double whammy," she replied. "Stick going home, and you're off. I can get Wednesday off if I ask. It's usually slow."

"What do you want to do?

"Whatever you want is fine with me."

"Let's see a movie," said Yoke.

"Solid."

They went to her apartment and stood at the door. Kaseya said, "You know how different you are." She paused. "Other guys know how to thrust themselves upon a girl to get what they want. You don't. At times I want to plead, but the way you act makes me want to follow your lead."

"I like to call it trust. Don't need force. All I need is your approval. No one can take that from you."

She smiled. "Melba isn't home."

"Neither is my heart," said Yoke. "It's with you. See ya tomorrow." They kissed, and he left.

* * *

Midmorning Tuesday at FBI Headquarters, Mr. Kent searched for a memo that urged the use of available bureau resources to aid agents in the field. He found the memo that assured funds for extended hours were available to the analyst. He heard a tap at the door. "Come in," he said.

Mr. Ward walked in. "Wanted to see me?"

"Yes," said Mr. Kent. "Thanks for coming. You will be compensated for this hour."

"Thank you," Ward said.

"See you got your crew coming in an hour late. And you covered for Yoke Wednesday night. Did he ask any questions?"

"Just why," said Ward.

"Good. His friend King will be in Tennessee sometime tomorrow. We need him to fill the void. Hopefully he gets his weekly haircut today, which will make his night easier."

"Why don't you tell him?"

"Too soon," said Kent. "Don't want to spook King. I'll tell him when my assessment of him is satisfactory. Besides, he knows we're watching King."

"What if Stick finds out and break things off with Yoke?"

"We'll deal with it," said Kent. "Tonight, have him clean the offices. Get a feel for him and let me know tomorrow."

"Sure will, Mr. Kent."

* * *

Yoke crawled out of bed at noon. He got dressed and headed for Mr. Edwards's barbershop. Inside, Mr. Edwards had a customer in the chair. When he saw Yoke, he said, "You're next."

One barber knew Yoke and Stick were friends. To provoke an issue, he said, "These young cats, making all that money, will spend it on friends before family."

"That ain't true," Mr. Edwards replied. "They take care of the family first; then they take care of the boys."

"Don't think Stick King is gonna make it," the barber stated.

"Why's that?" said Mr. Edwards.

"He ain't played against nobody."

"Well, he met with his agent yesterday."

"That's right, you know everything." He looked at Yoke. "How's things on Capitol Hill?"

"Don't know," said Yoke. "Don't work there."

"You mean you gave up that job?" asked Mr. Edwards.

"No, I was transferred to another agency."

"Is that right?" said Mr. Edwards. "Why?"

"Got into a little trouble. Can't talk about it."

Mr. Edwards popped his apron, dusted the customer, and massaged the man's shoulder as the customer dug into his wallet. He looked at Yoke and said, "Your turn."

Yoke sat in the chair, and Mr. Edwards pumped the chair to adjust it. After he wrapped his neck with toilet paper, he popped the apron and fastened it around his neck. Soon his clipper hummed.

"Heard you and Stick got into it with Herman and his boys," Mr. Edwards said.

Herman Ramsey was the hard-case man. He and a few of his associates acted as Shaw neighborhood watchdogs. Their major interest was Black traitors who wanted to keep Negroes politically sedated.

"Herman's crazy," said Yoke. "He called Stick a snake. He told Stick he could either get cut by Philadelphia or get cut by him. He even said they had their eyes on you, Mr. Edwards."

Mr. Edwards looked the shop over and said, "See what I mean? He's crazy. Don't believe nothing he say."

"But why you?" Yoke asked as Mr. Edwards tilted his head.

"He sees Whitey coming and going in my shop, but he doesn't know what's going on," said Mr. Edwards. "If Herman had a job, he would know what it's like to pay bills."

The other barber said, "But he scares me with all that militant talk. Talking about how they gonna take it to Capitol Hill."

"Yeah," Mr. Edwards replied, "heard about them having a campaign at the mall this summer. Have you heard about that, Yoke?"

"No, this the first I've heard."

"That's all they're talking about in church. Want Black folks to support the Poor People's Campaign."

The other barber said, "All that for broke folks. Talking about building shacks on the mall."

Mr. Edwards said as he edged Yoke's hairline, "Young men need to know when to be cool. Crazy guys like Herman—you can't believe nothing he say. So how can you be effective with people like that?"

"I'm satisfied with what I got," said Yoke. "But I do understand the need to help the poor. Maybe that's why Herman called me a snake charmer."

The shop broke into laughter. Mr. Edwards said with laughter as he brushed the hair off Yoke, "You sure are. He, he, he."

*   *   *

Yoke arrived at FBI Headquarters a little before seven. He was quick to notice that a few analysts were still in the office. He didn't think too much of it, especially, since Stick was out of town. His thoughts were focused on Kaseya and the evening they had planned for the following day. When Yoke went into the break room, he saw Gimme and Blue. As he put on his coveralls, Squirrel and Pearl walked in. Nutty arrived at seven. He rushed to get ready for the shift at the same time Mr. Ward wobbled in.

Mr. Ward said, "Yoke and Blue, hit the offices. Squirrel, Gimme, Nutty, and Pearl, hit the floors. Some of the analysts are on standby. Don't disturb them. Let's go to work."

At 11:00 p.m., they went to lunch. Yoke sat with Blue and said, "Don't see what the big deal is about." He wasn't going to let Blue know Stick was out of town.

"Don't worry," Blue said. "Every time they get jumpy, nothing happens. Just a waste of taxpayers' money."

"Bet it's good for the analyst," said Yoke.

"For them, yeah. For us, they adjust our schedule. The same problem the garbage workers are having in Memphis."

Mr. Ward said, "Shut your mouth before one of them hears you. Don't give no opinions and talk general."

Squirrel picked his guitar.

"Here we go again," said Gimme. "Man, give me some peace while I eat."

Pearl groomed his hair in the mirror inside his locker and said, "A little tunes won't hurt nobody."

Nutty said, "It will if he can't play."

Mr. Ward said with his mouth half full, "Cut it out. I got Mr. Kent to let you go at the regular time, and you'll get paid for eight." He spoke a half-truth. The late arrival and on-time departure were products of the director's implementation of more eyes and ears on the street.

The janitors cheered. Yoke said, "Thanks, Mr. Ward, for going to bat for us."

"Don't get all happy," he replied. "I can guarantee tomorrow night will be a different story."

*　　*　　*

Yoke picked up Kaseya at 2:20 a.m. She said, "Thought you were going to be late. Melba called and said she needed a ride home. Do you mind?"

"Naw," he said. "We got off on time. But he told us tomorrow will be a different story."

"You mean they are going to work harder because you're not there?"

"Don't think so," said Yoke. "The offices were still open when we left." It was the first time he thought, *Maybe Mr. Kent is using Stick for something else.*

"Every now and then, they have to justify their jobs," Kaseya said.

"That's right, but I don't think Stick is worth it. Even if he's going to the pros."

"They're following his money. And if he's not careful, he's going to go down."

"That's won't only kill his hopes; it'll kill him."

They motored to Club Madre.

CHAPTER 8

Wednesday morning was different. Mr. Ward stopped at Mr. Edwards's barbershop and sat in Mr. Edwards's chair. He said to Mr. Edwards, "The usual."

Mr. Edwards said as he prepared Mr. Ward for a haircut, "How's things in Hooverville?"

"Moody, as always," said Mr. Ward.

Eugene Battles, a barber, had been given the opportunity to rent a chair from Mr. Edwards. He had seen White men like Jake come into the shop but never ask for a haircut. Eugene had even told Mr. Edwards he could cut White men's hair. At best, he could give them a shave. He was never called upon to do so. The lack of confidence from his own people left a bitter scar. So he asked, "Did they send you?"

"No," said Mr. Ward. "I get a haircut every Wednesday. You should know that."

Eugene replied, "That's right. Mr. Edwards is on your payroll."

"Watch your mouth," said Mr. Ward.

Mr. Edwards said to Eugene, "Cool it. You're putting your hands in my pockets. Who do you think your customers are? They're government workers, fool."

"Whitey got you, but he doesn't have me," Eugene replied. Bet if you said no to him, your business would dry up."

"We all have been bought," Mr. Ward said. "We don't want to admit it. For example, what do you think of the two garbage workers that were crushed in Tennessee?"

Mr. Edwards said, "The machine shouldn't have malfunctioned. It's the city's fault. They always give Black workers their leftovers."

Mr. Ward looked at Eugene.

Eugene said, "The reason they were sitting on garbage was because Black workers aren't paid to work in the rain. White workers are. If the Black workers were paid, they would be alive today."

"All they gonna do is strike," Mr. Edwards said. "That won't make a donkey dance. You got to show 'em where you stand. By the way, this is Eugene last day with us. He's going to open his own shop. We'll see where he stands with the government."

Mr. Ward paid Mr. Edwards. "Keep in touch," he said.

*   *   *

Yoke was awakened by a knock at the door. When he opened it, Mr. Ward said, "light sleeper?"

"Naw, I was about to get up," said Yoke. "Don't tell me. I have to come to work tonight."

"No, you're still off," said Mr. Ward.

"Have a seat," Yoke said as he pointed at a chair.

Mr. Ward sat. "I stopped by to give you the title to your car." He handed Yoke the envelope. "Want to see if you understand your role as a janitor at FBI Headquarters."

"I understand," said Yoke. "Clean up, polish floors, and keep my mouth shut."

"That's part of it," said Mr. Ward. "The rest of it is your obligation to the bureau. We're used to augment the agents in the field."

"They want us to help them," Yoke said, "but they make it hard for us to become agents. Guess agent jobs are set aside for White boys."

"That's part of it," said Mr. Ward, "but you can't discount your value to the bureau. They rely on your help. This country relies on your patriotism."

"I don't get paid like agents," said Yoke, "so why do I have to risk my life for the same bullet?"

"It's not all about money," Mr. Ward said. "Everyone has at least one talent. It's up to him or her how he or she uses it. Your talent is being appreciated, but you're too bullheaded to realize it."

"What's my talent? How to keep my mouth shut?" said Yoke.

Mr. Ward said, "Your talent is analyze, process, and execute action, based on information received."

"So why am I off?"

"You're off because the director wants eyes and ears on the street."

"He wants information on how the ghetto feel about American issues. Right?"

"That's right, and that's your assignment for tonight. Report to Mr. Kent what you hear and see. It doesn't have to be anything spectacular. Just let him know."

"I'll do my best, but it's hard to do it when you're at the movies."

Mr. Ward laughed. "Thought you'd have an excuse. Keep your eyes and ears open. And remember the second word: 'disrupt.' That's all you have to do."

"Understood," said Yoke. "But Mr. Kent won't understand brothers' problems. We're frustrated. The government piss on us, and then they say they love us. We're poor because they want us to stay poor. That way they keep making money."

"Even though what you just said is true, that's just the way it is. Do your job, son. Do you think those poor bastards care how you feel about them? Believe me when I say this: if the shoe were on the other foot, they'd sell you out wholesale."

*　　*　　*

Wednesday afternoon, Mr. Ward walked into Mr. Kent's office. Mr. Ward said, "Stopped by Yoke's apartment. He told me he will let you know what he hears."

Mr. Kent stood behind his desk, looked out the window and said, "That's good he understands. Stick King is in Tennessee with his family. He can't provide the valuable intelligence Yoke can here."

"Why drag him along?" said Mr. Ward.

Mr. Kent said, "We operate off a budget. He was an unexpected expense. Got to make do with what we have. He fits the bill."

Mr. Kent's phone rang. He pressed a button and said over the intercom, "He's in Memphis at a strike. Sent you this message: 'calm and the rally is peaceful.' Don't know how ..."

"Thank you," said Mr. Kent. He looked at Mr. Ward. "We've done all we can do. Let's see if everything pans out."

*　　*　　*

Blue was cleaning one of the closed-door offices. He noticed that an analyst was still at his desk. He asked, "On standby?"

The analyst nodded. "Yes, I am."

While Blue emptied the trash cans, he noticed the desk was stacked with paperwork. The trash cans were overflowing, and the teleprinter ticked and clicked messages nonstop.

The analyst was from Tupelo, Mississippi—the same city Blue was from. His name was John Parker. Blue and John shared information frequently, but that night, John was reserved.

Blue asked, "If we can get over it, why can't the nation?"

"We're not trying to get over anything," John replied. "My job is to analyze. Why do more and get paid less?"

"Come on, John," said Blue, "We see the bull every day and can't say anything about it. Ain't that fishy?"

"It is, but we don't know the whole story. I would hate to act on something without knowing the full story."

"Is it?" Blue said. "You're just afraid of losing your job just like me."

"What are you talking about?"

"They transferred Carl, and Yoke showed up," said Blue. "They transferred Quid, and Squirrel showed up. And they transferred Slack, and Pearl showed up. We see what's going on."

"What do you see?" John asked.

"Every time a janitor outsmarts y'all, y'all take it personally. Maybe y'all not as smart as us," said Blue. "Admit it and shame the devil."

John got up, ripped the messages from the teleprinter, and said, "Information is like flour to a cake. Without it, all you got is scrambled eggs."

*   *   *

At the same time at Loew's Palace on 1306 F Street NW, Yoke and Kaseya watched Steve McQueen's *Bullitt*. As they walked to the car, Yoke said, "Man, I dig that mustang."

Kaseya said, "It's just a car and stunts. Don't get carried away."

"My car is the same, but I don't have the body," said Yoke. I'll show you."

They went to P Street, which was also known as Auto Row. There were many types and models to choose from. After browsing a couple of car lots, he saw a British racing green '68 Mustang fastback. The price was $4,468 dollars.

CHAPTER 9

The next afternoon, when Yoke arrived, the headquarters was busy. Analysts and agents walked from one office to another with haste. Yoke heard, "Twenty-two thousand students ..." and as he walked farther, he heard, "Oh no, a sixteen-year-old was shot by the police ..."

He went into the break room. Squirrel, Pearl, and Gimme looked nervous. But Blue—Blue was cool. He said, "Told y'all it was gonna happen."

"We're not supposed to talk about it," Nutty said, "So don't."

Mr. Ward wobbled in. "Blue, you and Yoke take the offices. Squirrel, Nutty, Gimme, and Pearl, the floors. Now cut the crap and let's get to work."

Yoke and Blue went into the closed-door office that now was wide open. The walls were uncovered, and the teleprinter ticked its existence. Paper overflowed boxes and wasn't ready to be taken away.

Agents scurried to piece together what had happened. From across the hall, Yoke heard, "Looting ..." He hesitated.

One agent shouted, "Get them the hell out of here!"

Yoke and Blue were ushered out, followed by a slammed door.

Yoke said to Blue, "What's up?"

"Tennessee is acting up," said Blue.

Yoke thought of Stick.

*   *   *

Gasoline cocktails flared through the air into stores. Fire hoses blasted water up and down the block. Windows were smashed, and looters collected made-to-order merchandise. Smoke from 150 fires scented with polyester, petroleum products, and wood hovered over the streets of Memphis. Stick and other students worked their way out of the chaos and into a calm zone.

Stick needed to get to a phone. The closest pay phone had been ripped from its pedestal. As he worked along his way, he noticed a policeman talking over his radio.

He said to the officer, "Need to talk to your dispatcher."

The officer said, "Get away from here before I run you in."

Stick scurried into the mob.

*   *   *

"Fifty folks hurt!" screamed Eugene in his new barbershop on H Street. "Twelve policemen injured. They're acting a fool down there."

Mr. Smith from Capitol Hill walked in and said, "Heard about your breakaway."

"You're right," said Eugene. "Park it in this chair."

Mr. Smith said as he sat, "Have you seen Yoke?"

"Yeah, at Edwards's," said Eugene. "That boy is confused."

Mr. Smith said, "What do you mean? He went to FBI Headquarters, and from what I hear, they like him."

"He's being used like the rest of you," said Eugene. "As long as they can keep that job, you won't go astray."

Mr. Smith said, "That's not true."

"Listen," said Eugene as he turned the dial on the radio.

Elijah Muhammad addressed his listeners: "The great problem of all time for the Black man in America is freedom, justice, and equality. War will be fought spiritually, not physically, by the God of Islam and his angels, who will use the force of nature ... Such will happen soon."

"Wow," said Eugene. "He's serious."

Mr. Smith said, "If you see Yoke, tell him to see me."

"Will do, but why?"

"Think he's getting a raw deal. He's a good kid, but the system wants to get to his type and destroy them."

"That's real stuff you're talking," Eugene replied. "Their talent is needed in the ghetto."

"That's what I'm afraid of—how they'll be used in the ghetto."

* * *

Yoke's phone rang. "Yeah, what's up?"

"This is Stick. Just got back from Tennessee. Me and some of the students got caught up in Memphis riot."

"What the hell you doing in Memphis?"

"We went to support the garbage men march," said Stick. "Man, things got out of hand. A bunch of young dudes called The Invaders started the trouble."

"Are you okay?" Yoke asked.

"I'm fine, but I'm not going back there. Pick me up at Melba's apartment."

"Is Kaseya there?"

"Yeah, she's here. See you soon, my brother."

"I'm on my way," said Yoke.

Stick hung up and said to Kaseya, "He's on his way."

Kaseya said, "Bet he wishes he had that Mustang. That man loved that car."

Stick said as he watched her from behind, "But in the meantime, I see you're getting fat back there."

Kaseya smiled. "Ask Yoke what he's been doing."

"Y'all ain't married," said Stick. "Let me tap that. I won't tell."

Kaseya was troubled. She didn't want to be intimate with him. At the same time, she was trapped with her emotions. Morning love is the best kind of loving. "Why me?" she asked. "Melba is a lot better."

Stick said passionately, "But Melba doesn't move me like you." He walked over to her and held her in his arms.

She refused to ward off her selfish feelings. She placed her hands on his shoulders and said, "Thought you were his friend?"

He said, "I am, but even Stevie Wonder can feel what I feel."

She said as he unbuttoned her blouse, "Promise me you won't tell."

"I promise," he said, and he kissed her.

When their lips parted, Melba opened the front door and walked in.

"When he gets here," Stick said, "let's go out for a late lunch."

"Come on, Kaseya," Melba said, "since you're already half undressed. Let's get ready." She went straight to her bedroom as Kaseya retreated to her room.

* * *

When Yoke picked up Kaseya, Melba, and Stick, Kaseya hugged Yoke with a tear rolling down her cheek. She said, "You don't know how glad I am to see you."

"Knew you would be," Yoke replied.

They went to Florida Avenue Grill. Inside the cramped soul food restaurant, they grabbed a table for four. When they sat, there was silence.

Yoke said to Kaseya, "What's wrong?"

"Nothing," she replied.

"Come on, Y'all. We don't have all day," Stick said. "I'm paying for this."

"What's new?" Melba asked. "You pay for everything."

Yoke said to Stick, "Why aren't you going back?"

Kaseya thought she was the reason. She believed he had fallen for her and believed she was in the process of falling for him.

"It's too violent. Black folks were grabbing everything in sight."

Kaseya thought, *Just like you.*

Melba said to Stick, "Found a new girl?"

"What?" said Stick. "Every time I turn around, someone is putting me in somebody's bed."

"Is it your imagination? Or is it your determination?" Kaseya asked. "Speak up for what you want. If you can't, leave it alone. I've got to go." She got up and went to the restroom.

"What's eating her?" Yoke said.

"Don't know," Stick replied.

Melba said mockingly to Stick, "Bet you don't."

"What's that supposed to mean?" Stick responded.

Melba said, "You cracked on Kaseya. When I walked in, y'all were all hugged up."

Yoke looked at Stick in disbelief.

Stick said to Yoke, "Look, man, we were alone. I made a play, and she accepted."

"How could you?" Yoke said. "I'm your main man. Like Nathan told King David, why did you have to have her?"

"Man, I'm sorry," said Stick. "How can I make it up to you?"

"tell you what. You pay for Melba's dinner, and I'll pay for Kaseya's." Kaseya returned to the table, and Stick said to Melba, "Come on, baby. We're going to eat somewhere else."

"You had to put your hands on her," Melba said.

"Look who's talking," said Stick. "I'm a man, and she's a woman."

"She's fragile and you know it. You screwed your friend to screw her."

Kaseya said to Yoke, "Still going to church Sunday?"

Yoke looked at her with disapproval but remained mute.

Stick said defiantly, "Me and Melba are going to Washington Cathedral. Ain't that right, babe?"

"Of course," said Melba, which meant Stick wasn't going to the club Saturday night. "Sunday morning, we're going to be some shouting fools."

Yoke and Kaseya walked out of the restaurant.

Stick said to Melba, "I'll make it up to him."

*　*　*

On the way to Missouri Avenue, Yoke asked Kaseya, "How could you go for Stick?"

She said, "He pushed the right buttons."

"Buttons? All I have to do is push a button?"

"You don't understand," she said. "He's faster than you."

"Didn't know I was in a heart race."

"You matter to me."

"Okay," Yoke said. "Tomorrow I'm taking you to meet my mother. Is that fast enough for you?"

"You picked up the pace," she said. "Baby, let's don't argue."

"Don't argue," he said. "My heart has been broken too many times. It's been three years since my last heartache. I've accepted it as being too young. Now you come along on a humbug, and I'm supposed to lie down?"

"Let me lie down with you," she said.

He clammed up and went to her apartment. He sat on the sofa while she made her way to the record player. She searched through her record collection and selected an album. She placed the needle in the groove of the Temptations' "Please Return Your Love to Me." She went to her bedroom. The album's last song ended just as she emerged into the living room. He looked her over and went out the door to take her to the club, after which he went home and got ready for work.

*   *   *

That afternoon, Yoke was pissed. He walked down the corridor, and when he passed one of the closed-door rooms, he heard laughter. An analyst said, "See you Sunday at Washington Cathedral."

Across the hall where Stick's picture hung on the wall, he heard, "He's not going back ..."

On Capitol Hill, the Friday before payday was considered rubber check day, so it wasn't a big deal. But this Friday at FBI Headquarters, the analysts and agents were relaxed. They acted as though their mission was accomplished. Instead of the deadpan personae, they were cheerful and, in some instances, cordial.

Yoke went into the break room. Janitors were laughing and joking. Mr. Ward walked in and said, "Let's get this shift over. The analyst was given a needed break for the weekend." He looked at a slumped Yoke and said, "Who stuck a finger in your honey pot?"

Yoke and Squirrel were assigned hall detail. As Squirrel swept, he said, "Gone be jamming on the strip tomorrow night at the Blue Mirror. Come on out."

"Ain't in the mood," said Yoke, but he knew it was on H Street across from Casino Royal.

Squirrel said, "Man, catch as many gigs as you can. Music has healing power. Wait, let me guess. Your girl left you."

"She didn't leave me," Yoke said, "She didn't cheat, but what she did showed she could be unfaithful."

Squirrel said, "She was testing you, man. She wanted to see how bad you want her. Bet she has a roommate."

"She does … so?"

Squirrel said, "They do it all the time. She is waiting for you to make a play on her roommate. Now tell me you did, sucker."

"Naw, I didn't, but tell me, how do you know so much about Black folks?"

"Been watching y'all, all my life," said Squirrel. "You need to let your heart bleed, bro. Let that crap out."

"What do I do?" said Yoke as he dipped his mop in the wax bucket.

"Look, my soulful brother," said Squirrel. "I bet she has beautiful eyes."

"She does," said Yoke as he swirled the wax from floorboard to floorboard.

"Well, my man, let me kill that heartache with my music. Come on out."

"If I'm not busy," said Yoke.

Squirrel's shoulders moved from side to side as he pushed the mop. "Let's get this stuff done. Heard Mr. Ward may let us off early."

*   *   *

Yoke's phone rang at 2:10 a.m. He walked in and answered, "Yeah."

"This Kaseya. I got a ride home."

Yoke said, "Let's get this straight. It's not me, but you. I should've known that the first time we met. I met you in a bootleg club full of hussies."

"Maybe," she said, and she hung up.

He decided it was too soon for her to see his mother.

Going to sleep on a heavy heart is weird. Sleep won't come, and neither will daylight. Time won't slip away, but the heart that doesn't give an upbeat keep pounding. Yoke loved her a day too soon. He should have known better. That's why he was hurt. He realized Stick traveled with a selfish soul.

He thought, *If the shoe were on the other foot, would I make a play for Melba?* He doubted the thought. The lesson he had learned, once again, was to not let anyone get under his skin. Yet he was a man of his word. If Kaseya was sincere, she deserved forgiveness for his mistake. *Never leave your woman with another man unless you're looking for a broken heart.*

*   *   *

Stick went up for a jump shot. Yoke nudged him in his ribs. He missed the shot. "Man, you're playing rough," Stick scorned.

"Not as rough as the Seventy-Sixers."

Stick said as he took the ball out, "Oh, so that's it. You're mad because she like basketball players. She wants a man, not a janitor."

Stick passed the ball in, and Yoke intercepted. He dribbled down court, and instead of laying it up, he paused in midair. Stick slapped the backboard, and Yoke laid it in.

"Next," Yoke said.

One of the other players said, "Y'all need to quit it. Playing like broke brothers."

Yoke snatched his gear and left. Stick said as he grabbed his loose gear and headed to the door, "He doesn't know how to handle a woman."

*   *   *

Yoke was driving home when he spotted Mr. Smith at Bargintown. He stopped and yelled out the window, "Need a ride?"

Mr. Smith looked at him and said as he smiled, "Man, I've been looking for you. Give me a ride, young buck." He climbed in.

"How's things on Capitol Hill?" Yoke asked.

"Same as usual," said Mr. Smith. "I want to talk to you about your transfer."

"Was I in trouble?" Yoke asked.

"Hell no," Mr. Smith said. "They ordered the move. Don't know what you heard or what you saw, but it scared the hell out of them."

"All they had to do was fire me. Instead, they watch everything I do."

"They're using you for their own benefit. Don't ever think for a minute they're on your side. Because they're not."

"What are you getting at?" asked Yoke.

"Sometimes we want to help others, but our wants are in the forefront."

Yoke thought of Kaseya and said, "Think I know what you mean."

"You think you're doing the right thing, but it only benefits you," Mr. Smith said. "That's not helping. It's hurting the ones who love you."

"I hear you talking."

"Don't let them talk you into becoming a Judas. You dig?"

"I dig what you're saying. I'm far from being a Sambo."

Mr. Smith looked straight ahead. "Are you?"

Once again, Yoke thought of Kaseya. Maybe she wanted to be sure. Maybe she was trapped in loneliness. Or maybe she was just a damn hoe. But at least he was in love with that damn hoe. The need for him to think things over began to surface. For the first time in his life, critical reasoning was required.

He dropped Mr. Smith off on Fourteenth and headed home. However, at the same hour, the former Bone-Crusher gang member Herman Ramsey was released from jail.

*   *   *

That night at The Blue Mirror, the Dead Puppies performed *Bette Davis Eyes*. As the song ended, Squirrel saw Yoke dressed in Capitol Hill causal—a sport coat and dress slacks—sit at the bar. Squirrel pointed at him as he sang the closing bars.

"Our next jam," Squirrel said into a microphone, "Is called 'Water on the Torch.' Enjoy."

He plucked into the instrumental introduction and picked up the cord to set the mood for the ballad.

He sang,

Mysteries belong to those who pray;
sunlight is for those who play.
But when Joseph died at war that day,
they knew on the porch.
Someone threw water on the torch.
Water on the torch.
Joseph's brother, John, one of our nation's greatest men,
came to look over us, but then
he was taken from us, and they knew on the porch.
Someone threw water on the torch.

Squirrel repeated the chorus with each measure focused on Yoke. He plucked his lead guitar into a solo with screams and howls.

After the set, he came over to Yoke and said, "See you made it. What do you think?"

"Pretty cool," Yoke said as Nutty walked over.

"How y'all doing?" Nutty asked.

"Cool, my brother," said Squirrel.

Yoke said, "They think we're looking for White women."

"Naw, bro," Squirrel said, "they want y'all to have a good time."

"Ain't nothing but a thing," Nutty replied, "So let's cool it."

Yoke said to Squirrel, "You made me think. Did I throw water on the torch?"

"You got it, my man," said Squirrel.

CHAPTER 10

Sunday morning, Kaseya didn't bother to wait at People Church's doors. She went in and took a seat on one of the side pews. The call to worship was ending when she saw Yoke sit on the other side. She smiled.

Yoke had figured she was at church, but his pride shielded his heart. He focused on Reverend Stanley as he stood at the pulpit.

Reverend Stanley said, "Today's word of God is The Children Are Crying ..."

Kaseya looked at Yoke and then returned her attention to the pulpit. Yoke's eyes searched the congregation and saw her on the other side. When he looked away, she looked at him. He, then looked at her. Now eye-to-eye, they realized it wasn't a coincidence. Neither of them wanted to blink first. Their attention returned to the sermon.

* * *

At the same time in Washington Cathedral, Stick and Melba sat close to the rear. The speaker spoke in his own time. There was no urgency, with there being no reason to convince anyone.

"I don't like to predict violence," Martin Luther King Jr. told the mostly White crowd of four thousand who packed the cathedral and spilled onto the lawn, one of whom was Herman Ramsey. "But if nothing is done between now and June to raise ghetto hope," King continued, "I feel this summer won't only be as bad as, but worse than, last year ..."

After the service, Stick and Melba made their way to Missouri. They walked in and found Kaseya on the couch, watching television.

"See Yoke today?" Melba asked.

Kaseya got up from the couch, rolled her eyes at Stick, and went to her bedroom.

Melba said to Stick, "Guess she didn't."

"Why worry?" said Stick. "I'll make it up to him."

"What about her? Told you she was fragile."

"They need to grow up," said Stick. "Ain't got time to babysit."

"Yeah, thanks to you. Think you'd better go."

"I'm gone," said Stick. "Is that fast enough for you?"

"Too slow," Melba said as she closed the door behind him.

She knocked on Kaseya's door and said, "He's gone. Come on out."

Kaseya walked out in her own time and said, "You don't understand. I don't have to grin at your sorry friends."

"He got the best of you, but do you blame him?" said Melba. "He's an honest man. He feels bad too."

Kaseya said, "A friend don't go around making a play for his friend's woman."

"It just happened," said Melba. "I'm not sore. The way I see it, lovemaking is just that—lovemaking. At least you had a chance to score with two guys."

"That's just it," said Kaseya. "The night Yoke slept here, we went to sleep in each other's arms, both of us naked, but nothing happened. He has a gentle soul. But his main man didn't see me as a woman. He saw me as a sex toy."

"Don't let your righteousness go to your head. Everybody in this town gets down. Don't let them fool you. I know. They cheat on their wives, and their wives cheat on them. That's the real world. Better come on in."

"No thanks, I'll take my chances," said Kaseya. "Yoke will be back. Wait and see. He'll be back."

*   *   *

After church, Yoke stopped at his mother's house. They sat at the dining table overlooking U Street. "What happened to you yesterday?" she asked.

"Had a busy day," he said. "Didn't want to trouble you."

"Trouble me with what? I'm your momma, and that counts for everything. Your problems are my problems."

"Mom, I met this girl, and I thought things were going to work out. But Stick tried to have sex with her."

"He tried but didn't. How's that a problem?"

"Don't feel I can trust her," he said. "She didn't strike me as that type of girl."

"So why do you go against your own judgement? I'll tell you why. Pride. She broke your heart, and now you want revenge. Think it over and give it some time. You'll see she's what you always wanted. I bet she feels the same."

"Saw her in church," he said. "She looked at me, and I looked at her. It was like a river we wanted to cross but didn't know how." Then he told his mother the most disheartening thing a mother could hear. He said, "I pray, but God don't answer."

She got up, walked into the kitchen, and said, "Did you thank him for putting her in your life? Bet you didn't. You thought you deserved her. What you must understand is that we don't deserve his blessings.

His blessings are given through grace and mercy. She didn't break your heart; you broke hers."

"How?" he asked.

"You left her at her moment of weakness. They were weak. She needed a strong man. She needed you." She turned around. "Y'all don't know how to swim. What are you waiting for? Bet y'all learn now. Don't wait too long, because when you do, it may be too late."

CHAPTER 11

Monday morning, Mr. Kent arrived at his office. As soon as he sat, his phone rang. "Mr. Kent," he answered.

"Mr. Kent, this is John. They can't agree. He's not going back because of the violence."

"What's the source?"

"ME 338-R," said John, "Also, ME 337-R and NE 110-R aren't talking. Communication has been compromised. ME 337-R claimed he did it to ensure NE 110-R would remain in focus. Since there aren't plans for a return visit, ME 337-R was put on standby."

"Thanks, John," Mr. Kent said. "Let me get NE 110-R back on track. In the meantime, keep me posted." Mr. Kent hung up, thought, *Iscariot*, and dialed Mr. Ward.

* * *

Herman Ramsey walked out of Eugene's barbershop. He made his way to Fourteenth and stood at the bus stop at Fourteenth and U. Yoke coasted to a stop.

Herman shouted, "Remember me?"

Yoke looked at him and then looked away. The last thing he needed was a scuffle before work. Besides, his heartstrings were nagging him. It was Kaseya. He missed her counting on him for rides to and from work. He missed her smile. He missed her eyes.

Herman said, "Man, you know I'm talking to you. Wise up, youngblood. Don't let him bring you down."

The light changed, and Yoke roared off. He wondered what it was between Herman and Stick. Not that it mattered to him. They were supposed to be out of his life. Now he realized he traveled on his word and nothing else.

*   *   *

Stick said over the phone, "No, I'm not going. Those folks are crazy. I'm too close to my dream for you to get me in some mess."

"Not telling you to go," Jake replied, "but be ready. Look at it this way; you don't want to go to Boston, but if you're in the playoffs, you've got to go. Be where I can reach you."

"Okay, man," he said before he talked in code: "Keep 'em coming."

"Yeah, yeah right. Heard you cracked on your partner's gal."

"I did, and I realize my mistake," said Stick. "He needs to cool off."

"Remember, Sanhedrin: don't mess this up. It was us who got you connected with the Seventy-Sixers. It was us that got you a Selective Service classification 2-A. Another way to put it, we're not interested in basketball. We're interested in Philadelphia. When you leave here, your partner will look after our interest in DC. Now, if you want out, I'll personally see that your classification is changed to 1-A and make sure you're drafted."

At that moment, Stick regretted letting Mr. Edwards talk him into doing business with Jake. He also regretted throwing Yoke's name on the table.

*   *   *

Mr. Ward reported for work at 5:00 p.m. He saw a note on their bulletin board that read, "See me, Mr. Kent." He snatched the note and went to Mr. Kent's office.

Mr. Kent said, "Looks like we are going back to normal. He's not going back, which means we can concentrate our effort on Operation POCAM."

"Yes sir," said Mr. Ward.

Mr. Kent went on. "Have Yoke see me when he comes in."

"Is he in trouble?"

"Naw," said Mr. Kent. "Need to talk to him. Think the time is right." Mr. Kent's phone rang. "Yes, what is it?"

The caller said, "Communication is still broken."

"Thanks," said Mr. Kent. He looked at Mr. Ward. "He's in trouble."

*   *   *

"Come on Kaseya," said Melba. "Ike is waiting."

"Coming, I'm coming," Kaseya said. She hustled out of her apartment and hopped into a Buick. As they traveled to H Street, Kaseya said, "Thanks, Ike, for the ride."

"No problem. What's a fine thing like you doing hitching rides? You should have your pick of all these hungry scoundrels."

"She does," Melba said. "They fell out and aren't talking."

"Already knows he's a fool," said Ike. "Baby, if that was me, I'd keep your drawers smoking."

"That's why you're not him," Melba replied.

Ike pulled up to Casino Royal and said, "If you need a ride, I'll have one of my lonely partners pick you up."

"Thanks," Kaseya said, and she looked at Melba. "I'll let you know."

"Her man must be funny and don't want nobody to know," Ike said. "She's too fine not to be getting tapped."

Melba replied, "She's too fine to fool around. That's her problem."

* * *

Monday afternoon, when Yoke reported for work, he walked into a happy mess. He heard, "They're divisive ..."

The first of the month was relaxed on Capitol Hill, but at FBI Headquarters they were crazy glad.

Mr. Ward approached him before he got to the break room. "Mr. Kent wants to see you."

"Am I in trouble?"

"As usual but relax. They're relaxed today."

"Never thought the first of the month meant so much to them."

Mr. Ward said, "Go on and see what he wants."

Yoke did an about face and went to Mr. Kent's office.

* * *

Inside Casino Royal, Kaseya said, "What can I get for you?"

The man said, "Been off today. How about a whiskey sour?"

"Whiskey sour it is," said Kaseya.

Before she could walk away, the man said, "Yoke will be fine too."

She rolled her eyes. "I fetch whiskey, not men."

"Want to help your man and help you in the process."

"Excuse me, what is your name?" she asked.

"Eugene Battles, owner of the new barbershop. Used to work for Mr. Edwards. Tell him I need to see him. It will benefit both of you."

Kaseya turned and went to the bar.

* * *

Yoke went into Mr. Kent's office. "Have a seat," Mr. Kent said. Yoke sat.

"What's this I hear about you and Zezebee King?"

"I'll tell you who to ask," said Yoke, "ask Stick."

"Stick doesn't have to know you're his backup. We need you to patch things up with him. He has already offered an apology and is willing to make it up to you."

Mr. Ward said from the corner, "Don't be hardheaded, son. Forgive him and let's move on."

Yoke looked from Mr. Ward to Mr. Kent. "If that were your wife, would you do it?"

Mr. Kent stood from his desk and said, "It doesn't matter what we would do. All that matters is that you do what you're told."

Mr. Ward added, "You got a gravy life ahead of you. Don't let that man ruin it."

"At least give it some thought, said Mr. Kent. "Look around. Everyone is happy. Join the fun. We never know when things are going to be good again."

"Is that all?" said Yoke. "I've got floors to sweep."

"Don't wait too long. There are other janitors ready to take your place."

Yoke walked out.

"He'll either conform or rebel," Mr. Ward said.

"If he rebels, God help him," Mr. Kent replied as he threw his thumb over his shoulder. "Jesus is behind me in line."

*　　*　　*

Stick was out and about. He checked on Melba and then made his way to Casino Royal. There he looked up Kaseya. Eugene was still there and was joined later by Herman Ramsey. So, when Stick walked in, they were quick to notice.

"There he go," said Eugene.

Herman swiveled. "Lady Luck is on our side."

"Hold on," said Eugene. "Don't start no trouble here. Let's see who he talks to."

Stick made his rounds and ended at the bar. Kaseya came to the bar to order drinks. He pinched her arm. "Sorry."

"Sorry?" she said. "Sorry? What about Yoke?"

"He's tougher than you think," said Stick. "He'll get over it, and y'all'll be kicking it again. Watch what I say." He felt a tap on his shoulder.

"You're holding up our drinks, my man," Herman said.

"You again," said Stick. "What's your problem?"

"Our problem is you." He walked back to the table.

Stick said to Kaseya, "I should've stayed in Tennessee."

"Melba told me," said Kaseya. "She thinks you came back for me."

"Look," Stick said, "what happened, happened. You don't want me any more than I want you. Put it on the shelf."

She smiled. "Tell Yoke that."

Eugene and Herman got up to leave but saw Stick sit at Ike's table.

Eugene said to Herman, "That's the waitress's ride. He's going to hook her up with that guy. That's how he thinks."

"Yeah," Herman said, "that's the proof. If he sells out his friends, you know he'll sell us out. Gonna get that punk. Don't care if he's going pro."

CHAPTER 12

Tuesday morning, Yoke broke his usual routine. At the same time, he committed a critical error. He went to Eugene's barbershop for his weekly haircut. The barbershop wasn't sanctioned, in that information from government employees wasn't supposed to be discussed there.

As Yoke entered, Eugene said, "Welcome, my brother. My chair has been waiting for you."

"Number two and a shave," Yoke said.

Eugene prepared him for his cut. At the same time, Herman walked in.

Herman said to Yoke, "All Black people aren't for all Black people."

"Man, you're always talking crazy," said Yoke.

"That's what they want you to think," Herman said. "I've figured them out."

"Bring him on in," Eugene said.

Herman said to Yoke, "You think I'm a hard-luck case. The government made sure I'll never be a credible witness."

"Preach on, brother," Eugene said as he trimmed.

"When they know you've figured them out, you become a threat," Herman said. "Control is the name of the game, baby."

Yoke said as Eugene tilted his head, "Being paranoid won't solve nothing. We got to survive. You can complain all you want, but the truth of the matter is this is the way."

"Way to what?" Herman asked. "Hell? That's all you gonna get. Unless … unless you say the hell with this and make a change."

"What are we trying to change?" said Yoke. "Forgive them for they know not what they do? Forgive your girlfriend because she betrayed you with a kiss? Be sacrificed for the good of the whole? Now who's brainwashed?"

"That rat there is the problem," Herman replied. "You're scratching for cash because the White man told you that's the best you're gonna do. But he doesn't tell you; he learns from you every day."

"Ah, come on, man," said Yoke. "Get a job and stop blaming the White man."

Herman spoke curtly. "I'm not blaming the man. I'm pointing out his evil intent. All you must do is accept being inferior, and all your troubles will go away, right? You sweep their floors, but they won't let you get close to management. You dust their desks, but they won't allow you to have one. You even lie for them because they know you don't know any better. Most of all, they can get you to spy on yourself, your mama, and your friends."

It was at that moment that Yoke began to piece things together. He said, "You're calling me a traitor because I work for the government?"

Herman whispered, "Shoe fits, wear it."

*   *   *

Kaseya wrapped her robe tight. Her hair was wirily tossed. The oven was warm, and the frying pan on top of the stove was hot. She walked to the window to check the weather. There was a slight overcast with the sun beaming through. A Pontiac was parked across the street with two silhouettes in the front seats. The phone rang, and she answered. "Hello?"

"This Ike."

"Stick is here. Want to talk to him?"

Ike paused.

"He's in bed with Melba," she said.

"Want to see you this morning," Ike replied. "Can you make it?"

"Maybe," she said. "You want to see me because I'm weak."

"How you figure?"

"When I wanted him to fill my need, he was shy. I need to be loved, and you know it. So yesterday I gave up. If he doesn't want me now, I'll understand."

"Forget him," he said. "He's the least of your worries. Come with me. Like I told you, this time I want you with me."

"The least you can do is beg," she replied.

"On bended knees."

"I'll be ready in thirty minutes."

"I'll be there in twenty-five."

She looked out the window and saw the car still parked outside. For a split second, a woman's face appeared and glimpsed at her bay window before it retreated into the shadow.

Stick came out of Melba's room and said, "Need to grab a couple of things." He then left.

* * *

Yoke left the barbershop and headed toward Missouri. On his way, he saw Stick get into a Cadillac, and it pulled into traffic behind him. The odds of the Cadillac traveling in the same direction was high. After all, Melba lived on Missouri. So Yoke made the first right turn, and the Cadillac turned too. He made another right turn, and the Cadillac traveled straight toward Missouri. Yoke gave up and made his way home.

Stick said to Ike, "That was close, man."

"Thought you said they were finished," Ike replied.

"They are," said Stick, "but he may be having second thoughts. I want to see Melba before I fly home. After you and Kaseya drop me off at Dulles, y'all can hang out."

Ike said as he turned onto Missouri, "Don't need no hassle, brother."

"It won't be no hassle," Stick said, and Ike drove past the parked Pontiac. He parked in front of the apartment complex.

Stick's plan was simple. He wanted Ike preoccupied with Kaseya so he wouldn't make a play for Melba while he was gone. Kaseya would never fall for a woman-rambler like Ike.

He handed Ike a twenty and said, "This should be enough for gas and Kaseya today and tomorrow. I should be back Thursday afternoon."

*   *   *

That afternoon, Mr. Kent got a phone call. He said, "You're clear."

The analyst stated, "ME 337-R is going back."

"For what reason?"

"To shadow him. He'll be back Thursday."

"Who is going to take his place?"

"No one," said the analyst, "but if it makes you feel better, we got approval for NE 110-R to fill in."

Mr. Kent said, "Don't need to let him off. We don't expect any trouble."

The analyst said, "In that case, over and out," and he hung up.

*   *   *

Later on, Tuesday afternoon, Yoke got ready for work. Since he didn't have to take Kaseya to work, he took his time.

As he drove on Fourteenth, he saw Kaseya and Ike window-shopping. The sight of her with that guy hit him in the gut. He turned the radio up and cruised.

*   *   *

Kaseya noticed when they left her apartment that the Pontiac drove off. Now on Fourteenth, she looked around and saw Yoke as he passed them. When they got back to the apartment, she saw the Pontiac pull up and park across the street. She went inside while Ike waited in the car.

Kaseya emerged from her apartment in an overcoat. She got in, and Ike pulled off. The Pontiac trailed them to Casino Royal. She got out, went inside, and hustled to the front window. She looked down and saw the Pontiac pull off and follow Ike's Cadillac.

*   *   *

As Yoke walked down the corridor, he noticed analysts scrambling from one room to the other room across the hall. As he got closer, he overheard an analyst say, "… Invaders started it …"

Once again, the serious deadpan faces had returned. They were no longer cordial. It was business as usual. When he stepped into the break room, he said to Blue, "Tired of the mood swings around here."

"This ain't nothing," Blue said. "Wait until tomorrow. You'll see."

CHAPTER 13

Wednesday morning made no promises to Yoke. He got up and headed for the corner grocery store. On his way, he saw Jake in front of Mr. Edwards's barbershop. He continued and noticed Herman and a couple of men on the other side of the street. Their attention appeared to be drawn to Jake. He scanned the street and noticed there was no Stick.

He parked, got out, and went inside the store. He heard a man say to the clerk at the cash register, "It'll all end in violence. People are angry. You can't talk your way out of that."

Yoke got a gallon of milk and went to the cash register.

"How angry are you?" the clerk asked.

"Not angry at all," said Yoke. "This city is too big to stay pissed off." The clerk rang up the milk.

* * *

Kaseya was worried. She had expected something to happen when Ike and Melba showed up, but it had gone without any glitches, even when Ike walked her to the door. Nothing. It was a good thing they hadn't kissed. Yet, she had entertained the thought, *it was better to catch the bus than to catch rides with Ike*

She looked outside, and there wasn't a Pontiac in sight. She tapped on Melba's door. No answer. She called Yoke, and again there was no answer.

*　　*　　*

Stick arrived at his parents' house. "Back again?" His mother said.

"Yeah, had to come here for a class assignment," he replied.

"The professors at Howard are really into sociology."

"Yes ma'am," he said. "Easy grade. I flew, but the students should be here within an hour."

"Where are you going?"

"To the Masonic Temple, Church of God in Christ," he said. "Then I'm flying back to meet my scout tomorrow afternoon."

*　　*　　*

Kaseya walked out of her room and went straight to the fridge. She poured a glass of orange juice, went to the front window, and sat. There was no Pontiac in sight. It was a fair day with nothing to anticipate except for some of her sleazy customers. It was an easy day; in that she wasn't in love. It was a moment she could truly concentrate on herself.

Melba came out of her room and said, "Another day, another dollar."

"If money makes your day," Kaseya responded, "you're in sad shape. The jobs we have are only temporary. Don't know about you, but as soon as I get my change right, I'm gone."

"Do what you gotta do," said Melba. "Either way, I'll make the rent and expenses."

"There you go again asking about the rent and expenses. I pay my share, and I believe you can find someone to take my place. Who knows, with any luck, they may like working at Club Madre."

"What about Ike?" Melba asked. "You gonna leave him hanging?"

"He's just a friend, not my husband. Don't have any commitment to him."

"What about Yoke?"

"He's yesterday's news," said Kaseya. "He's probably not even thinking about me."

"I think he's trying to find a way to get over you, but he can't."

"Whatever you say," said Kaseya, "I've got to move on." She looked out the window and noticed the Pontiac. "Is Ike gonna pick us up?"

"Of course. He'll be on time."

*　*　*

Mr. Kent said to the director over the phone, "Everyone's in place."

"Good," said the director, "Don't need any screw-ups. Monitor the evening's events and report your findings to me. We have transcripts of last Sunday's Washington Cathedral. Our source got access to his speech for this Sunday—'Why America May Go to Hell.'" He hung up.

Mr. Kent realized there was no love lost between the director and his target. Yet Mr. Kent believed the only way his program was to succeed was if it focused on the mall. It was a couple of months away from when demonstrators were scheduled to arrive. He called Mr. Ward.

After a couple of minutes, Mr. Ward tapped on the door and said as he entered, "Need me?"

"No need to do the floors in the offices," Mr. Kent replied. "They're going to be working late tonight. And don't worry about the teleprinters. I'll be around until ten."

"Yes, sir," said Mr. Ward, "I'll have Yoke and Blue do the sensitive rooms."

"Sounds good to me. We're going to shift our efforts to Operation POCAM. Think we got things under control with Stick's whereabouts." He stood and looked out the window.

"You've been head of GIP for a year." Mr. Ward said as he wobbled and sat. "What do you expect to get out of it?"

Mr. Kent turned from the window, sat, and held a ballpoint pen to his lips. "Intelligence through surveillance."

"Seems to me it's sad when a country spies on its citizens."

"GIP was formed to gather intelligence in the hope that we can be proactive to prevent riots like Watts."

"Sounds like it has good intentions," said Ward. "May I remind you Malcolm X was under heavy surveillance by an undercover police officer, and he still got killed. How could that happen if you're trying to be proactive?"

Kent leaned forward. "No matter how many policemen are on the street, if a man is determined to kill another man, it will happen!" He sat back and went on. "That's why our mandate is to 'discredit and disrupt.'"

"So, what you're saying," said Ward, "GIP isn't about protecting citizens; it's about control."

Kent said, "If you say so."

"Well, it appears there's only one benefit from surveillance," said Ward.

Kent straightened in his chair. He dropped his elbows on the desk and, with braided fingers, asked, "What's that?"

"Regardless of who's doing the surveillance, somebody gonna get killed. That's what happened to Malcolm X and President Kennedy," said Ward.

Kent sat back. "I don't make the rules."

"But you waddle in it," said Ward, "like a pig waddle in feces."

*   *   *

Time clicked on. Again Yoke found himself not in a rush. He was beginning to feel he had been too harsh on Kaseya. After all, he didn't blame Stick, who was at fault. After he got ready for work, he decided to drive by Kaseya's to see whether she was all right.

*   *   *

Ike arrived on time to take Melba and Kaseya to work. He walked into their apartment and said, "All aboard. This plane ain't waiting on nothing."

Kaseya came out of her room fastening her overcoat. "I'm ready. Better ask your friend."

Melba walked into the room. "What's the rush? Every time you get in a hurry, you come too soon."

Kaseya looked out the front window and saw the Pontiac.

*   *   *

Inside the Pontiac, the woman driver said, "He's in there, Mary. He claimed he just gives them a ride to the club."

"Janice," Mary said, "I think you're going overboard. He's not going to let those hussies mess up his good thing."

"Let's wait and see."

Janice was Eugene's cousin and Herman's childhood friend. She had heard about Stick through them.

"That Stick is a low-down brother," said Janice.

"He's doing what he has to do to get by."

"And he does it well. He's a sellout brother. Herman told me; they're gonna get him."

*   *   *

A few minutes earlier, Yoke took the long way to work and stopped at a corner store to buy some gum. It was the same store where Kaseya shopped for spur-of-the-moment items. After he paid for his gum, he stepped outside and noticed a Pontiac turn onto Missouri. He got into his car and took his time before he pulled into traffic.

*   *   *

"Let's go," Ike said.

Kaseya opened the door. "Melba, why don't you let Ike drop me off first since you're not pressed for time."

Melba yelled from her room, "Y'all go on down and warm up the car."

Ike looked at Kaseya and shook his head. They left the apartment and strolled to the car. Ike unlocked the passenger door and opened it.

Kaseya saw two women get out of the Pontiac. One woman stood at the car and looked around before she caught up with the driver.

Janice said to Ike, "What the hell is this?"

"Nothing, baby. Just giving them a ride to work."

"Who are 'them'? All I see is her."

*   *   *

Melba looked out the front window and saw Ike's wife shouting at him. Then she saw the pistol.

*   *   *

Yoke looked down Missouri and saw a woman with a pistol pointing it at a man and Kaseya. He whipped onto Missouri and roared to her apartment.

*   *   *

Janice shouted, "Y'all think I'm a fool. You're screwing her."

"You got it all wrong," Kaseya said.

Janice aimed at Kaseya and pulled back the hammer.

"Baby," said Ike, "Don't make a big mistake."

"Baby?" said Janice. "Who are you talking to? Me or her?"

Melba stood at the window and waited. If she went down to the car, his wife would put two and two together. Melba also noticed that a small crowd had started to form.

Yoke's tires screamed to a halt in the middle of the street. He jumped out and yelled, "Kaseya, what's going on?"

She slowly moved to Yoke, and he held her in his arms. She said, "I need a ride."

"Come on," he said, and they got into his car.

"See," Ike said, "I told you there was nothing between us."

Melba stepped outside.

"Really?" said Janice.

Yoke and Kaseya roared down Missouri. She turned in her seat to look back. *Pop-pop!* Ike fell to the sidewalk through a cloud of smoke. "She shot him." She turned around in her seat. *Pop!* In her mind, she felt that final bullet must have been for Melba. Yoke picked up speed.

On the way to Casino Royal, not one word was spoken. Yoke pulled in front. Before she got out, she didn't even say thank-you. She jumped out and ran into the building.

*   *   *

Kaseya went straight to the bar. Jack poured her a glass of wine and slid it before her. One waitress said, "Some woman just shot a man on Missouri Avenue. Caught him messing around."

Another waitress asked, "Who?"

"Ike," she said. "I think his wife shot the woman too."

Jack noticed Kaseya break into tears. "Was that your ride?" he asked.
Kaseya nodded.

"Did y'all have anything going on?"

She shook her head.

"Then it's not your fault. Don't worry, I'll give you a ride home."

* * *

Yoke kissed his crucifix. There was nothing he could do to
rationalize his reluctance to speak to Kaseya. He felt he didn't have to.
She had made that bed, and now she must lie in it.

As he walked down the corridor, Mr. Kent saw him and said, "In
my office."

Yoke stepped into the office while Mr. Kent stood at his office
window. "Have anything to report?" Mr. Kent asked.

Yoke believed Mr. Kent had heard about what had happened on
Missouri Avenue. At this point, he didn't care what action Mr. Kent
was going to take.

"What do you know about ME, NE, and listening posts?" Mr.
Kent asked.

"Nothing, sir."

Mr. Kent continued to look out the window. "ME means 'mission
essential.' NE means 'nonessential.' Listening posts are places in the
community that are vital to our communication. Do you have anything
to report?" Mr. Kent wasn't ready for the answer.

"A man was shot on Missouri."

Mr. Kent whipped around. "What?"

"A man was shot on Missouri, and I think his girlfriend was too."

"How do you know?"

"I was there, sir."

"What were you doing there?"

"I have this woman I like. I drove to her place to see if she needed a ride."

"Is this the woman that you think cheated on you?"

How did he know? Yoke thought. "Yes sir. She's the one. I saw a woman with a pistol, my girl, and a man by a Cadillac. I picked her up, and while we were on our way, I heard three shots."

"What did you do?"

"Nothing, Mr. Kent. Nothing. Just took her to work."

Mr. Kent sat. "What did you talk about?"

"Nothing, Mr. Kent. She jumped out and went to work."

"Good," said Mr. Kent. "You and Blue are going to clean a sensitive office. I know you and Stick are friends, so don't get alarmed by what you hear."

"Yes sir," said Yoke. "Will that be all?"

Mr. Kent stood. "That's all, son. And thanks for letting me know what happened."

Yoke was the last one to walk into the break room. It was business as usual—the same bland conversations and the same boring routine.

Blue said to Yoke, "We got the room tonight. Analyst John is from Mississippi. Should be an easy night for us."

Mr. Ward overheard Blue and said, "Not really. Mr. Kent will be in the room too."

*   *   *

At the Masonic Temple in Memphis, Stick called Melba and got no answer. He called Club Madre, and a lady said, "She's not here."

A student said, "Come on, man. Let's grab a seat.

What Stick didn't know was that his solution to make things better with Yoke had just parked at 422½ S. Main Street.

*   *   *

Mr. Kent rolled up his shirt sleeves and loosened his necktie. Headphones were clamped on Analyst John's ears as Mr. Kent stood over his shoulder in the booth. Yoke and Blue entered the office to retrieve the trash receptacles.

John said to Mr. Kent, "Talking like that, you sure won't."

Mr. Kent cradled his chin before he looked through the glass wall at the custodians. He said to John, "He's working the people."

Yoke picked up a trash can close to the booth entrance and heard John mumble, "Liar ..."

Mr. Kent looked at Yoke and pointed his head toward the office door.

Yoke said to Blue, "Hurry up and let's go. We got to go across the hall."

"I'm on it, my man," Blue replied. "We're ahead of schedule."

* * *

Kaseya was busier than a rambling hen. That was good. It kept her mind off Melba. Eugene and Herman walked in and sat at a table. Eugene waved her over.

"What can I get for you?" she asked.

"A couple of beers," Eugene said. "And where's Stick?"

"Don't know," she said. "He's not my man."

"He got my friend in a lot of trouble," Herman said, "and I don't appreciate it. You should know—"

Eugene butted in. "You dated my cousin's husband."

"We never dated," she said. "He gave us a ride home."

"Janice saw you with him the other day and then you came home and got dressed for work. Who do you think you're fooling?"

"No one," she said. "Need to get your orders." She did an about-face and headed for the bar.

At the bar, Jack said, "Trouble?"

"Two creeps think I was dating Ike."

"Need me to have them thrown out?"

"Naw," she said, "I can handle them. But I still need a ride home."

Jack pushed two beers to her. "You got it, babe."

* * *

In the break room, Yoke said to Blue, "Be glad when this shift is over."

"Me too," Blue said. "Did you have a lousy day?"

"The worst in years," Yoke said. "Think I heard two people get shot."

"You mean you were on Missouri?"

"Right in the middle of it," he said. "Knew the girl and gave her a ride to work."

"What happened?"

"Guess the man's wife or girlfriend caught him."

Blue said, "The girl you took to work, was she dating that guy?"

"Don't know," he said, "and didn't ask. We didn't talk, and when we got to the club, she jumped out and ran inside. I saved her butt and didn't even get a thank-you."

Blue laughed. "Real heroes don't do it for thanks; they do it because it's what's right."

"I did it because I still have feelings for her," he said, "and I didn't like the sight of a gun pointed at her."

Blue dropped his sandwich. "Did you tell Mr. Kent?"

"He already knew."

* * *

Kaseya didn't bother to call Yoke. Jack took her home. When she got out of the car, she saw a bloodstained sidewalk. She went into the apartment, but there was no blood. She tapped on Melba's door, and there was no answer. She went to the phone and called Club Madre, and she was told, "She didn't come in."

Her next thought was to call the police for a report on what had happened. She dialed DC Metro.

A desk officer answered. "Is this an emergency?"

"No sir," she said. "Need information about the incident on Missouri yesterday afternoon."

"Sorry Ma'am can't give out any information on an open investigation," he said. "However, if you have any information pertinent to the case, we'll be glad to sit down and discuss it."

"Want to know," she said, "was anybody killed?"

"Not allowed to discuss it," he said, "but if you come in and cooperate, I can assure you peace of mind."

"Thanks. If I hear anything, I'll let you know."

"Thanks for calling." He hung up.

At least for now, no news was good news for Kaseya.

* * *

It was a long shot, but Yoke waited for Kaseya to call. It was two-thirty in the morning. He rationalized she could have called while he was on his way home. To be truthful with himself, maybe she wasn't interested. All he was doing was racking his brain over a matter he couldn't control. He got into his pajamas and lay on the bed.

CHAPTER 14

Thursday morning, Stick and a couple of students headed for Canipe Amusement Company, a record store at 424 S. Main Street. As they approached the store, Stick took notice of a Mustang coupe as it pulled to the curb. That's when it occurred to him that Yoke was crazy about mustangs. It parked in front of the record store. As he got closer, he saw a clean-shaven, well-dressed White man get out with a six-pack of Schlitz. The man was about the same height as Yoke.

"Hey, man!" Stick yelled.

The gentleman looked at him, stopped, and waited.

Stick said, "That's a nice car."

He looked up. "Thanks."

Stick offered a minor embellishment. "I'm Stick King, drafted by the Seventy-Sixers."

"That's great. Good luck." The man turned to leave.

"How much do they cost?"

He smiled. "It'll set you back about twenty-five hundred." He turned and walked into Bessie Brewers at 422½ S. Main.

* * *

Yoke got dressed to step outside. He climbed into his car and turned on the radio. It played the intro to a song and went out. He thought about what Mr. Kent had said—"nothing fancy." The radio had to break before payday. He switched it off, drove to the store, picked up a loaf of bread, and returned home. The moment he walked in; the phone rang.

"This is Stick."

"And?"

"Look man, we need to get over this childish stuff. I know I made a mistake." He wanted to know whether Yoke had seen Melba but didn't know how to ask.

"I'm finished with the whole thing," said Yoke. "Took Kaseya to work yesterday." He stopped at that point. He didn't want to be the one to tell Stick Melba had been shot. So he said, "Haven't seen Melba. Kaseya been catching rides with cats I don't know."

"If you see Melba," Stick said, "tell her I'll be back this afternoon."

"I will if I see her," Yoke replied, "but I'm not going out my way." He hung up.

*   *   *

Stick knew he was wrong, but he called Kaseya.

"Hello," she said.

"This Stick. Is Melba there?"

Kaseya didn't know what to say. She didn't want to give up on Melba. "Haven't seen her since yesterday."

"What about Ike?" he said to see how things were going.

"Last time I saw him was yesterday. Yoke gave me a ride to work. But I've been getting a ride home from Jack, our bartender."

"Okay, when you see her, tell her I'll be home this afternoon." He hung up.

*   *   *

"Well son," said the auto mechanic, "think you got a blown radio tube. I checked the fuse box, and everything was good."

"How long will it take?" Yoke asked.

"As soon as I can find a used radio."

Yoke got into his car and left. On his way home, he saw Jake on a pay phone.

* * *

Stick said to Jake over the phone, "Need an advance of three thousand."

"Money isn't the problem," said Jake. "The problem is your report."

"Report what? Nothing happened."

"Are you sure? Seems to me something happened on your home front."

"What now?" said Stick. "Who shot John?"

"Close. Meet me in an hour for your money."

"Now you're talking my language," said Stick. "Want to make it to P Street this afternoon."

"Buying a car?" said Jake. "Wait until you see the whole deal."

"I will, but the car is for my friend. I'll meet you at six."

"It will be cheaper if you guys kiss and make up."

* * *

Eugene sat in a coffee shop with Herman's eyes on him. Herman said, "It's not what you do, but how you do it."

"He hooked her up with that man to break them up," Eugene replied.

"Maybe," said Herman, "but he had a habit of screwing around. Janice couldn't change that."

"He thinks he can get away with anything, but his butt belongs to me."

"What are we going to do?"

"He gets money from that White cat Jake every Thursday. We'll catch him this afternoon."

"And then what?" said Herman.

"I'll cut his throat."

"That's pretty harsh for screwing around."

"No it's not. He's a sellout, and everybody knows it. Mr. Edwards got the goods on him. He knows he's not a brother."

"What do you need from me?"

"Bust his head wide open," said Eugene.

"It's done. Get him this afternoon."

*   *   *

It was three o'clock that afternoon. Kaseya had walked to the candy store and returned to her apartment with a newspaper. The moment she stuck the key into the door, she heard the phone ring. She hastened to open the door quickly, but by the time she made it to the phone, the caller had hung up.

The phone rang again, and she answered. "Hello?"

"This Jack. Got to set up early, so be ready at five."

"No problem." She hung up.

She scanned the local section and found the article that reported yesterday's shooting. It stated a man was wounded by his wife on Missouri Avenue and was expected to recover. But it didn't mention Melba. That was unsettling. *Maybe her next of kin haven't been notified.*

She called Club Madre. "Is Melba there?" she asked.

A lady answered. "No."

"Could you have her call Kaseya when you see her?"

"Sure, honey," she said, and she hung up.

*   *   *

At four o'clock that afternoon, Yoke was confused. The more he thought about Kaseya, the more he resigned to his thoughts of her. Perhaps he was being too hard on her. After all, Stick was a player. If Yoke had been more careful, Kaseya would still be his companion. He lost his Capitol Hill job, lost Kaseya, lost Stick, Melba was probably dead, and now his damn radio didn't work. What else could go wrong? When he looked in the mirror in his bathroom, he had to admit he was a terrible screwup.

He started to call his mother but realized she had gone to his brother's house in Boston. He turned on the radio and went to get ready for work.

*   *   *

At five o'clock that afternoon, Herman met Dean at the corner of Fourteenth and U. "He usually meets that White dude every Thursday afternoon," Herman said.

"Why are you doing this for Eugene?" Dean replied. "Janice should've known better. It's not your fault she got sloppy."

"It's not about Janice," said Herman, "It's about that traitor, Stick. They got him into the pros."

Dean said, "Who are 'they'?"

"The Man, that's who," said Herman. "Look over there. See him, that White dude? Why's he going into Mr. Edwards's barbershop?"

"For a shave."

"They don't cut White guys' hair. He's going there to clear things with Mr. Edwards," Herman said. "Something is going on between them."

"You're a nervous wreck. Need to relax and let it be."

"We've been slack too long to let things be," said Herman. "Gonna set things straight." He stuck his hand into his pocket.

*   *   *

It was five-thirty when Yoke left late for work. The traffic was heavy, but he managed to arrive on time. As he walked down the corridor, he heard, "… dinner at …"

*   *   *

Kaseya walked into the club ballroom. Tables were beginning to fill. She said, "Let's start now," and she moseyed over to the first table.

*   *   *

Herman said to Dean, "What's wrong with you?"

"Jones, brother Jones."

*   *   *

Stick left his dorm room and made it over to Fourteenth. He crossed it and met Jake at Mr. Edwards's barbershop. Jake handed him an envelope and said, "Better know what you're doing."

"I do," Stick replied. "Do you know what you're doing?"

"I do," said Jake.

It was then that Eugene appeared.

Eugene walked up and said, "Well, well, the gang's all here."

"Gene, my main man," said Stick, "what's with the don't know?"

"You screwed my cousin," said Eugene.

"She had it coming."

"Just like you," said Herman.

* * *

At 6:40, Yoke entered the break room. Blue said, "They're crazy talking about how busy the analysts are. When they busy, it holds us up."

"Are they working late again?"

"You got that right," said Blue. Mr. Ward was called into Mr. Kent's office just before you walked in. Didn't you see him in the hall?"

"No, I didn't," said Yoke.

Blue laughed. "Bet Mr. Ward's bowlegs scrambled like a rooster."

Mr. Kent rushed into the break room followed by Mr. Ward. Mr. Kent said hastily, "Need all of you to go home and report tomorrow at eight in the morning."

Yoke didn't dare to ask what was going on. He and the rest of the janitors got up and hustled out of the building. Yoke noticed in the corridor that agents and analysts were scrambling into offices. He got into his car and made his way to the Shaw neighborhood. It was 7:45 that evening.

* * *

On the corner of Fourteenth, Eugene walked from Stick, leaving him with Herman and Dean. Stick said to Eugene as he walked away, "I was out of town when your cousin got into trouble."

Eugene kept walking and turned the corner. Herman said, "That's a good excuse. But this isn't about Janice; this about you."

"Oh," said Stick. "Your Black militant beliefs."

"You and Mr. Edwards joined the wrong side," said Dean, "That's all."

Herman rudely replied, "Y'all are selling your people out for money. Even Judas had enough sense to hang himself after he betrayed Jesus for money. But since you're not thinking about suicide, let me help you." He reached into his pocket and pulled out a razor.

*   *   *

Across the street at Mr. Edwards's barbershop, A graduate from Howard and a band of students stepped in. "Stokely," said Mr. Edwards, "good to see you."

"You need to close your shop out of respect like you did for President Kennedy." He and the students left.

Mr. Edwards switched the dial on the radio. He closed the shop, looked across the street, and saw Stick talking to Herman. It was five after eight that evening.

*   *   *

Yoke traveled down Fourteenth and noticed a crowd, which was unusual for a Thursday evening. He approached Mr. Edwards's shop and noticed it was closed. He looked across the street and saw Stick standing tall against a razor-wielding Herman. He whipped in front of the barbershop, parked, and hustled to his trunk.

He got a lug wrench, pointed at Herman, and yelled, "He's with me!"

Herman and Dean turned and started to walk toward him. Yoke turned around and hurled the lug wrench end-over-end into the barbershop window. Herman and Dean stopped in the street, and for a moment, there was silence. After that, store windows were smashed on both sides of the street. It was as though a human wave of Black folks roared down Fourteenth, leaving destruction in their path. Herman and Dean hustled to join them.

Yoke yelled to Stick, "Come on; let's go!"

* * *

Kaseya walked to a table to take their orders. Four White men chain-smoked and trembled. It was obvious they would soon be in a hurry. She realized it when they ordered beers. Mixed drinks would take longer. She saw the manager walk to the front window, look, and hustle back to Jack at the bar.

* * *

Yoke turned off Fourteenth to make his way to H Street.

"Where are we going?" Stick asked.

"Pick up Kaseya."

"We're on Fourteenth," said Stick. "Let's work our way along and pick up Melba."

Yoke didn't want to be the one to tell Stick she was dead. He played it off by saying, "You're right. Let's get her." His strategy was to let Stick find out himself.

They maneuvered around looters on Thirteenth who were making their way from stores. He could hear sirens from a distance. He managed to work his way back onto the 2200 block, which was ahead of the riot path. He said to Stick in front of Club Madre, "Hurry up; they're headed this way."

Stick jumped out and ran inside. The noise was increasing. In his rearview mirror, he saw flames and the crowd approaching the block. He looked out his window and saw Stick and Melba cross the street.

They hustled to the car. Stick jumped into the front seat, and Melba jump into the back.

Yoke looked into his rearview mirror and said, "Where you been? Kaseya is worried about you. She thought you got shot."

"Wait. What y'all talking about?" said Stick.

"While you were gone," Melba said to Stick, "Ike's wife tracked him down at our place. When I came out, she had a pistol and looked at me. When she said, 'Really,' I walked like I didn't know Ike and went up the street."

"We heard three shots," said Yoke.

"She shot Ike in the kneecap and thigh. Guess she wasn't satisfied and shot him in his other thigh."

By now they were approaching Casino Royal, but the rioters were dead on their trail. He pulled to the front and saw Kaseya and Jack hustling to the parking lot.

Yoke stood halfway out the door and yelled, "Kaseya!"

Stick got out and yelled, "Kaseya, over here," and he got in the back with Melba.

Kaseya turned around and hustled to the car. She hopped in, and they took off.

Kaseya turned in the front seat and hugged Melba. "Why didn't you call me?"

"Called today, but you didn't answer."

"Where were you?" said Kaseya.

"Went to Silver Spring yesterday. Figured if that crazy woman knew where I lived, she would know where I worked. But she got arrested, and so I came back to work tonight."

"We'll go to my place tonight," Yoke said. "Got a double fold-out sofa for Stick and Melba."

Kaseya said to Yoke, "Turn on your radio."

"It's broke," said Yoke.

Stick smiled. He knew he had the solution, and he was going to solve it by the weekend. He had the money for Yoke's Mustang.

"But what's going on?" Yoke asked.

"Martin Luther King was shot and died at five after eight," Kaseya said. It was five after seven in Memphis.

The moment they walked into Yoke's apartment, he went straight to the radio and turned it on, after which he pulled the cushions off and unfolded a bed frame from the couch. Kaseya and Melba sat at the tea table near the window. Stick sat in a chair. All the while, the radio blasted the developments in Memphis.

Yoke said to Kaseya, "You can change in the bedroom. Think I have a shirt and pants that will fit. Wear them until we can get to your place tomorrow."

Stick said to Yoke, "Hope things settle down. Need you to take me to Auto Row tomorrow morning."

Melba kept her ears and her attention on the radio. Yoke made the couch, and Kaseya found something to wear. It was around 8:25. Melba said, "Listen to this."

A reporter said, "The authorities are on the lookout for a well-dressed White male about five feet ten inches and one hundred sixty to one hundred seventy-five pounds. The suspect was last seen in a late-model white mustang."

Stick sat back in disbelief. He'd had a conversation with him about the Mustang that morning in Memphis. He needed to give Jake a heads-up.

"And you did nothing?" Yoke said.

"He was cool, calm, and collected," said Stick. "He didn't stand out. Let me use your phone."

Yoke cocked his head and said, "Sure, put a dime in the ashtray."

Stick bumped Yoke as he walked over to the phone. He lifted the receiver, and as he was dialing, he said, "That's your problem. You don't have any ambition to get rich."

"And I won't," said Yoke.

"Boys, give it a break," Melba said. "King was shot, and y'all still in the ghetto doing ghetto things."

Yeah," said Stick on the phone. "This morning when I was in Memphis, I spoke to the guy." He paused and listened. He then said, "See ya tomorrow," and he hung up.

* * *

Yoke stepped outside into the smell of smoke-filled air. Stick and Melba followed him. Kaseya waited at the door.

Yoke said to Stick, "Catch ya tomorrow after work."

Stick held Melba close. "We'll be back." He turned and left.

Yoke went back inside.

"I'm tired," Kaseya said. "Let's go lie down."

"I'm right behind you," said Yoke.

* * *

The next morning, Stick met Jake in front of Mr. Edwards's barbershop.

"Well, what was he like?" Jake asked.

"He was cool and collected," said Stick. "He was well mannered."

"Most murderers are," said Jake. "He didn't want you to make him., so he treated you like one of them rather than a nigga." Jake smiled.

"Hey," said Stick, "That's not funny. Anyway, I noticed he was a sharp dresser. We talked about his car. He wished me luck with the Seventy-Sixers."

"What a sport," Jake said. "He played you and didn't skip a note. Well, I don't see any problem with that."

"Why's that?" Stick asked.

"After what happened last night," said Jake, "I heard a rumor we're shutting down our operation."

*   *   *

In June, after Robert Kennedy's assassination, Yoke went to work and noticed that both secret rooms were vacant. The door plate on Mr. Kent's door was bare. Later that day, he was instructed to report to work at the Capitol.

Kaseya was called back to the Department of Commerce. Melba stayed close to Stick, but since he was out of town, she spent most of her time at the club. It was business as usual.

Even though Stick said he'd be back, he never showed.

*   *   *

By now it was August 1968 when Stick went to the practice facility for the 76ers training camp. The moment he stepped into the locker room, a guard coordinator said, "Dr. Jack wants to see you."

He went to the office that had Jack Ramsay Head Coach on the name plate. He opened the door and went in.

Coach Ramsay said, "Have a seat." Stick sat. Ramsay went on, "I have a difficult decision to make. Shaler Halimon is nowhere the player you are but he's a strong forward. I have Clark as a guard with two years' experience; Greer as a guard with ten years, and Jones as a point guard with four years. So you can see, you as a guard isn't what I need. If you can wait about three years and if Greer retires, perhaps I can give you a fair shot."

"What are you trying to say Coach?" Stick asked. "I didn't make the cut."

"You didn't," said Ramsay. "You're a player with great potential. So, here's what I'm going to do. I'm going to call Coach Pedro Ferrandiz of the Real Madrid basketball team. They were last year winners in the FIBA in Europe. I'm going to put in a strong recommendation. As for now, you're released from the 76ers. Best of luck."

Stick stood and left the office.

*   *   *

Yoke browsed the Sports Illustrated and strolled the NBA teams. Under Philadelphia 76ers, China Lee King wasn't mentioned. He also checked their roster and sawStick never made the 76ers roster. Melba also lost contact with him. None of them knew his whereabouts.

*   *   *

That was the turbulent 60s. Yoke heard a conversation that could've destroyed his dream. What Stick saw destroyed his basketball career. Kaseya and Melba thought they could talk their way through life. The FBI thought the Ghetto Informant Program (GIP) was an effective tool to control the Black masses. None of them ever considered the inevitable: Nothing can escape the fishbowl.

NOTES AND REFERENCES

Glick, Brian. *War at Home.* Boston: South End Press, 1989.

Malloy, Courtland. Interview with Odessa Madre. *Washington Post, 1980.*

Stanley, A. Knighton. *The Children Is Crying.* Cleveland, Ohio: Pilgrim Press, 1978...Smashwords

Wikipedia, s.v. "COINTELPRO," last modified October 27, 2021, https://en.wikipedia.org/wiki/COINTELPRO.

Wikipedia, s.v. "Ghetto Informant Program," last modified June 3, 2020, https://en.wikipedia.org/wiki/Ghetto_Informant_Program.